TALI NOHKATI
THE GREAT CROSSING

KOZA BELLELI

Dear Susan,
Enjoy the crossing
with Tali,

Koza Belleli

Black Rose Writing | Texas

ISBN: 978-1-68433-258-8
PUBLISHED BY BLACK ROSE WRITING
www.blackrosewriting.com

Printed in the United States of America
Suggested Retail Price (SRP) $15.95

Tali Nohkati is printed in Plantagenet Cherokee

Translated into English by Dorine Heller

To Esther and Jude Lejba

− CONTENTS −

TALI NOHKATI
THE GREAT CROSSING

– PART ONE –

« In Beauty happily I walk
With Beauty before me I walk
With Beauty behind me I walk
With Beauty above me I walk
With Beauty all around me I walk
It is finished in Beauty »

Strophe of Kledze Hatal, Navajo shaman chant

1 AT THE BEGINNING

It happened a long time ago.

In those days, the Moon was alone in the sky, and Coyote was alone on Earth. In total darkness, they wandered around like lost souls.

When he could no longer hold back, Coyote said to the Moon:

"Sweet friend, we cannot keep on living like this forever."

"You are right, things need to be different," the Moon answered.

Without further ado and incessantly, they started to work; doing, undoing and redoing. Was it the fruit of their labor, fate or just luck? Days and nights slipped by in an instant.

For companionship in the sky, the Moon scattered the Stars and the Sun.

On Earth, the big ocean appeared. Mountains emerged. Soon, Coyote was traveling through the plains, discovering trees, animals, and all the flowers of Creation.

Seeing all this beauty around them, the Moon and Coyote felt deeply happy.

As Coyote wandered along the banks of a river, the soft clay, stuck under his paws, took the shape of a human being. A man and a woman stood before him.

It was the beginning of a new age.

Shortly thereafter, a child was born from the union of these two beings. His mother, his father, the Moon and Coyote looked at him with much love and announced the news far and wide.

Day after day, they marveled at his eyes, his nose, at the delicate folds of his ears. But, to them, the most charming thing of all were his small feet. They would not stop tickling them, nibbling them. And the child shrieked with laughter.

This is why they named him "Tali Nohkati", which means 'two feet'. And that is how this nickname became his name.

Life went on, peacefully.

But, alas, it happened... It happened that a blazing wind swept up everything in its path.

Nothing could stop the deadly strikes of lightning and the frantic procession of flames. Everything was burned away: the trees, the animals, the flowers, as well as the man and the woman.

Several days passed, and only a few twigs and smoldering carcasses laid strewn on the ground. Having survived this disaster, Coyote and Tali Nohkati huddled up against each other at the very end of the cave, trembling with terror.

The Moon, who had searched for them for a long time, finally found them. Once Tali Nohkati, exhausted, had fallen asleep, the Moon said to Coyote:

"What a great tragedy! What will become of that child, now that his parents are gone?"

"I do not know. But, for now, do you have any food for him?" Coyote asked.

"Only enough for a few days," the Moon answered. "Afterwards, I will have nothing."

"In that case, the child will have to leave," Coyote said. "Far, far away from here."

The Moon looked at the ashes-covered landscape and said, with a reassuring tone:

"I have seen some lands, beyond the horizon, which have been spared. Tali Nohkati should be on his way, with these leather hides and these provisions."

When Tali Nohkati woke up, Coyote was standing by his side. Faced with the despair and the surprise of the child as he looked at what the Moon had left him, Coyote explained:

"There is no more life here. There is nothing but desolation. You will have to leave."

"Leave! But to go where?" Tali Nohkati asked, with a sob.

"Beyond the horizon," Coyote answered. "There, some lands have been spared."

"Will you come with me?" Tali Nohkati asked.

"How could I? I am not and will never be one of your kind. My paths are not and will never be yours. For all that, I will not abandon you. When our paths cross again, I will know how to find you, and when you need help, call my name. I will surely hear you."

Tali Nohkati had no choice but to comply. As Coyote, who had given him a few embers and a handful of dried herbs, watched him with saddened eyes, he put his hides on, took the provisions and walked away.

Soon enough, his frail silhouette disappeared and Coyote, struck by great distress, howled into the night as it wrapped up the world.

2 YUPIK, THE SHE-BEAR

Tali Nohkati walked for a long time, under a low and grey sky. The white frozen ground that cracked under his footprints stretched out endlessly. Never had he seen such scenery.

His eyes, once bathed in brightness and colors, grew accustomed, day after day, to the pale light. On high alert, his senses sharpened, enabling him to face the hardships of his new life. Thanks to the fire, which he succeeded in maintaining, he withstood the lethal wind, which ruled supreme over this land.

However, the provisions, which the Moon had left him, became scarce.

One morning, racked with hunger, Tali Nohkati noticed a movement on the ice. Moving carefully as to avoid the crunch of ice, he approached slowly and, lurking low against the ground, he saw a bear.

The immaculate coat of the animal merged with the snow. Yet, Tali Nohkati soon realized that it was a she-bear and that, on her side, was her standing cub.

Afraid that they would notice him, Tali Nohkati stayed still. He watched them for a while. They must have been hungry as well for he saw the she-bear position herself in front of a waterhole. On the lookout, she was pawing the waters. All of a sudden, she caught a big fish, which she immediately gulped down. She pawed the water again, and another fish landed on the ice. The cub took his turn and devoured it.

How fascinating it was for Tali Nohkati.

"How clever," he thought. "As soon as they leave, I will do the same."

But it was a rich spot! And so, the she-bear and her cub, seemingly guarding the entrance to a miraculous cave, settled down to snatch all that would wriggle.

Finally sated, the cub fell asleep next to his mother. The latter watched over him. She tenderly licked his muzzle, when, looking up to search the horizon, she saw a strange shape, not so far from her.

Intrigued, she moved away from her offspring for just a moment to inch closer to Tali Nohkati.

The latter trembled with fear. Puzzled, the she-bear walked around the unknown body, sniffing at the leather hides.

She came closer, looked deeply into the eyes of the child and, with frankness, asked:

"Are you cold, is that why you are all curled up? Are you hungry, is that why you look so thin?"

Stunned, Tali Nohkati did not dare to answer. Then, mustering all his courage, he confessed:

"It is true that I have been walking in the wind for a long time and that I have no more to eat. It is true that I am tired and that my stomach is more and more of a pit every day."

With those words, the moved she-bear offered:

"In that case, come with me. My name is Yupik. I have a whole stock of fresh fish and seals. My breasts are full of nice, warm and rich milk. In the White Land, loneliness is deadly. You would not survive it."

Tali Nohkati grabbed the soft coat of the she-bear. Guided by her, and along with her cub, he soon found himself coiled up within her lukewarm flank.

This shelter turned out to be of great value. Indeed, a raging storm caught the three of them by surprise. Huddled up against each other, they resisted the storm comfortably. Once the sky had cleared up, revealing its intense blue, Yupik introduced Tali Nohkati to her cub, Qanuk.

Qanuk happily welcomed his new playmate. Sliding and rolling, Qanuk, once the weather cleared up, convinced Tali Nohkati to come and play with him. The latter was thrilled at the idea of playing and allowed himself to be led into the new field, one he looked at with new eyes.

But Yupik, who was watching their every move, called them to order. Under the gusts of wind and the snow flurries, the providential waterhole had vanished. Now with two mouths to feed, the wise she-bear wanted to leave promptly in search of sustenance. With a heightened sense of smell, she resumed her journey, with Qanuk and Tali Nohkati on her heels.

Soon, Yupik stopped on the verge of an arm of the sea, freed from ice, and walked along the edge of the banks before leaping into the water. When she came back to the surface, her sharp fangs were tearing the flesh of a seal, desperately but to no avail trying to break free. She dealt a final death blow to the seal and offered the prey to Qanuk and to Tali Nohkati.

Qanuk, excited, approached to devour the fresh flesh, but Tali Nohkati stayed back. Yupik, noticing that he was not eating, asked him:

"Is the view of all that blood repulsive to you?"

Tali Nohkati did not dare contradict her.

"Still you will have to eat," added Yupik. "Even if you cannot stand this truth, in order to survive, you will have to sacrifice other lives. It is the way it works. Soon, I will not have any more milk. When the fish is scarce, other preys are sufficient. Before long, as I did for Qanuk, I will show you how to hunt."

Tali Nohkati joined them. He kneeled down close to Qanuk and partook the best pieces that Yupik had left them.

Yupik had a lot of patience. Fortunately, because it is not easy to initiate and neither is it to educate.

Undoubtedly, Qanuk and Tali Nohkati were very good students. They burst with enthusiasm, but Yupik had to correct their clumsiness. Some of it would bring terrible consequences: they could get lost and not find a shelter or help. Therefore, they had to remember their lessons well, and often, during recess, Qanuk and Tali Nohkati took advantage of the time and practiced what they had just learned.

As they were practicing a fishing technique, a big bear passed by. Since he was the spitting image of Yupik, Qanuk and Tali Nohkati did not worry about his presence. But Yupik knew too well what she had to fear. It was not uncommon for a solitary male to fall on a cub. Jealous, violent and vindictive, he could grab him and ruthlessly kill him.

Even if this one was just watching them out of the corner of his eyes,

Yupik gathered them up and decided it was safer to walk away.

Walking on the ice was full of surprises. The White Land had one thousand and one faces and Tali Nohkati, in spite of the harshness of his new life, was often filled with wonder.

After a long absence, the Sun finally returned. Its light, evolving along with the days, made the snow and the ice sparkle. When the sky, streaked with grey, darkened, the crystalline icebergs brightened the horizon or turned into threatening shadows at dusk. Those gigantic blocks played with the sea, capturing the indigo of the waves, creating a dreamlike scenery of extraordinary beauty.

At times, Tali Nohkati, Yupik and Qanuk would come across some partridges, foxes or penguins. But those encounters were rare. The warm season, too brief in this country, compelled each and every creature to deal with basic necessities and be cautious.

Yupik knew it too well, one had to catch before being caught.

With the arrival of spring, the snow melted and entire walls of ice drifted towards the open sea. The land, more alive, came into bloom.

Their steps led Tali Nohkati, Yupik and Qanuk to the ocean. Yupik knew that it overflowed with vast resources, so she decided to settle there for the entire summer.

From then on, Tali Nohkati knew that he could find enough to eat under the ice, but he still had to learn how to hunt with his own hands. Yupik had saved his life when she took him in, but he could not help thinking of the moment when he would have to leave them and resume his journey. The warm season would give him the chance to gather his strength and sharpen his skills.

Although the sea was an excellent source of food, it was not necessarily docile. Its waves were strong, with frightening creatures swimming along its shores, and Tali Nohkati, unlike Yupik, could not dive into the cold water.

Luckily, he found the remains of a washed-up whale on the sand. It had been long since the birds and the crabs had devoured the flesh and stripped the ribs of the animal.

This sight brought back memories to him. He recalled his father's gestures when he was fishing in the river.

Tali Nohkati thought: "That could be the framework of a small boat." He got down to work, gathered sealskins, stretched them out to build a hull. He tied up several branches, also washed-up, in order to make paddles and fish-traps.

Finally, making the most of a lull, he took it out and paddled beyond the waves. The waters of the bay were generous. The barely submerged fish-traps filled up. He came back loaded with fish and shared his catch with Yupik and Qanuk.

Throughout the endless days, the Sun was beating down. It would glide on the horizon and run its course again. Tali Nohkati watched it doings when the Moon, without warning, landed on his shoulder and whispered:

"I knew I would find you here. How happy I am to see you again!"

"Moon! Moon! You came! Coyote is not with you? How did you know I was here?"

"From my celestial vault, I can hear the sound of your voice, I can catch a glimpse of you sometimes."

And, stroking the cool cheeks of the child, she added:

"I knew that you were very brave. I said it to our friend, whom I came across the other night and who thinks of you dearly."

Suddenly, she shivered, curled up on the neck of Tali Nohkati and asked:

"You did not light a fire?"

"How could I? My embers were blown away by the wind. Here, the land overflows with water, the wood is scarce, and the flames would scare my travelling companions away."

"I understand," the Moon said, looking at Yupik and Qanuk sleeping.

The emotion of this unexpected encounter overwhelmed them. They stayed quiet for a long time, cheek against cheek. The Moon eventually broke the silence:

"What will you do when Winter returns? Will you linger in the White Land? Far away, I saw some lands, covered by majestic trees along rivers. Often, I have contemplated them."

"Where are they?" Tali Nohkati asked.

But he could not hear the answer. The Moon had already left.

Yupik, once awake, saw Tali Nohkati on the shore. She approached, tenderly licked his hands and invited him to follow her. Yupik did not like it when Tali Nohkati was alone. When the Moon went back to the sky, she released a few opals. Tali Nohkati saw them, so different from the stones that covered the ground. He took them in his hands and, remembering her, brought them close to the warmth of his heart. Then, he left to go fishing. The sea, like a mirror, reflected the skies. With gentle paddle strokes, Tali Nohkati glided on the waters. He got ready to throw his fish-traps when he noticed a huge fish swimming along with his boat. Fear took hold of him. Not daring to move, he observed the animal. The fish, however, was placid, seemingly floating between the waves. A strange blow escaped from this enormous mass. Tali Nohkati did not know what to think. Was it a sign? Was it a call? All of a sudden, the beast turned on her side. With her eye, she stared at the child and said to him:

"Take your boat further out. Not far away from here, there is a school of shrimp."

Tali Nohkati could not believe his eyes nor his ears. "What should he do?" he wondered. "Follow the beast? Rush back to Yupik?"

Amused by the child's daze, the whale swam around the boat and pushed it ahead to the swarm of krill. After the fish-traps filled up, she took back Tali Nohkati, still stunned, to the shore, expelled air and disappeared into the depths of the ocean.

Yupik and Qanuk knew Atii the whale very well. Often, she would play with them. At times, they would even hear her sing. When Tali Nohkati told them what had happened, Yupik and Qanuk reassured him. They knew that there was nothing to fear. Never, never had Atii hurt them.

From that day on, the whale would accompany Tali Nohkati when he left on his boat. She would position herself close to the shore, protecting Qanuk from the deadly attacks of the leopard seals and of the killer whales.

The summer slipped by. They all ate their fill. The mild weather created some good hunting and fishing. Yupik got plenty of fat in reserve, Qanuk grew, and Tali Nohkati felt lucky.

Yupik was basking in the Sun when Tali Nohkati noticed, a few steps away from her, the silhouette of the big bear. He did not worry. Within the quietness of the day's end, immersed in his work on the boat, he even forgot his presence. The big bear, however, inched closer. Facing the wind and dozing off, Yupik could not detect his smell. At this very moment, the bear acted. He grabbed Qanuk, who was wandering along the outskirts of the shore. He snatched him, fastening his fangs in the still tender flesh. The growls of pain from Qanuk alarmed Yupik. She rose up in front of the bear and tried to free the cub from this ferocious grasp.

Tali Nohkati grabbed some stones and threw them, aiming at the head of the animal. Besieged, the male finally released Qanuk who, covered in blood, fell to the ground. Yupik was enraged and pounced on the male bear. A violent fight started between them.

Tali Nohkati took advantage of this moment to find shelter for Qanuk and help him with his wounds. He thought about starting a fire to scare away this ruthless enemy, who had loomed up from nowhere. Alas, there was no wood. Still, he grabbed some clumps of grass and rubbed two stones against each other. Suddenly, the grass, soaked with the grease of the sealskins which had dried on it, caught fire. Poked by the wind, the fire spread rapidly, giving rise to a wall of flames that grew between the sea and the land.

Exhausted by the relentless attacks from Yupik, and surprised by the violence and the power of the fire, the bear let go. Defeated, he ran away, his body gashed by claws strokes and bites. Yupik ran to Qanuk, exhausted as well. But the view of the fire terrified her. Little by little, Tali Nohkati calmed her down, reassured her with soft words, petting her. Yupik understood that this powerful fire would create a shield. It would be their best defense. She let go, trusting the arms of Tali Nohkati and tried to save Qanuk. This terrible test did not undermine the confidence of Tali Nohkati and Yupik. As for Qanuk, deeply wounded, he drew from their tenderness and from the resources of his youth to recover his strength. But they all knew that they had come within a hair's breadth of death, and that the coming winter would constitute an even stronger enemy.

Already the first blanket of snow was coating the rocks on the coast, when Yupik told Tali Nohkati:

"It is time for you to resume your journey. Soon, the night of the White Land will fall. Qanuk and I are going to fall into a deep sleep and we will not be able to share anything with you anymore. What will you do then, sheltered in your igloo?"

"Nothing worthwhile," Tali Nohkati answered. I was dreading this moment but I must accept it. The Moon told me of trees and rivers, but where would those lands be?"

"Probably more southwards. Atii the whale, who will leave before the Sun disappears, will know how to take you there."

"Oh! Yupik! Yupik! Damn be the winter that tears us apart!"

"We will greatly miss you," the she-bear confessed. "You have been a wonderful brother for Qanuk. Thanks to you, I found again the firstborn that I had lost. You have been our beloved companion, and we owe you our lives."

As he was listening to her, Tali Nohkati was crying. The idea of this separation hurt him. Yet, he knew that it could not be any other way. He had to resume his journey.

The biting cold whipped his face. As he had done in the past, Tali Nohkati embarked upon a new journey, carrying with him his weapons and his meager luggage, his embers and his courage.

3 ATII, THE WHALE

Atii the whale, left without further delay, knowing that the ice field would soon imprison the waves.

It proved to be priceless to be by Atii's side. Without her, he would have lost his way. Carried by the currents and led by her instincts, she guided him through the maze of icebergs. Thanks to her advice, the child did not lack neither fish nor shrimp. The catch, grilled on the embers, would be delicious. Its aroma would attract birds flying in the wake of his small boat.

The labyrinth of ice was very dangerous. Often narrow, its jagged points stuck out ominously. Tali Nohkati had to ensure that none of them ripped open the sides of his frail skiff. The labyrinth was also of rare beauty.

Its translucent walls shimmered in the sun, draped in glints of blue. They were, for the sea and for the sky, the altar of their union. Under the rays of the Sun, which paved the way to the south, the turquoise and the indigo crashed together, creating iridescent patches and bringing to light the pearl white of the snowflakes. Frozen inside these ice cubes, they looked like captive pearls in a glass box.

A softer breeze began to drift, and the polar scenery slowly vanished. The ocean appeared in all its vastness. The gaze of Tali Nohkati leapt into infinity.

Suddenly, a school of beluga whales approached. The whiteness of their skin reminded him of Qanuk and Yupik. The child's heart sank, but his new companions filled him with joy. For the first time, a sense of power flowed through Tali Nohkati. Life's surprises and wonders had touched him.

Atii, happy to see her protégé in awe, led this procession far, far away into the night.

Tali Nohkati, lulled by the waves, fell asleep and woke up as the new dawn lit up the sky. Atii greeted him with her kind eyes and said:

"Up there, on the ocean, waves are forming. Do not worry. I will stay by your boat and... "

But Atii did not have time to finish her sentence. Without any warning, the storm crashed down in full force. The swell strengthened. The troughs of the waves manhandled the boat. Tali Nohkati tried his best to stay on course. Alas! His strength alone was not sufficient, and the fragility of his hull did not resist the battering of the breakers.

The frail skiff tore apart. Water rushed in. Tali Nohkati, seeing himself being swept away, tried to grab a hold of the scattered debris. However, the currents drowned all of his hopes. For a moment, thinking he was seeing his wreck, Tali Nohkati grabbed one of Atii's fins. But to no avail. His hands, stiff from the cold, slipped from the monumental body of the whale and Tali Nohkati sank.

Out of the blue, Atii, who had not lost sight of her protégé, pulled him towards the surface so that he could catch his breath. Then, opening her mouth, as she would do to swallow her food, she gulped down Tali Nohkati.

The child found himself in the depths of Atii's throat. This sudden plunge into darkness left him confused. The inside, warm and humid, was also odd. Although he perceived the jerks of the storm raging outside, Tali Nohkati could also hear the heartbeats of the animal. It was like a faint reminiscence of the journey which, in the past, had led him to his birth.

All of a sudden, everything became still and quiet. Tali Nohkati's thoughts were driven into a chaotic jumble. Unsettled, he did not dare to move in this gigantic body that he did not know. He perked up his ears, attempting to pick up the slightest noise. But nothing, nothing could be heard except for that soft heartbeat. Atii perceived his fear and said to him:

"Make yourself at home, Tali Nohkati. Go wherever you'd like."

This voice resounded so loudly that it startled him.

"Where do you want me to go?" he asked, stupefied. "I cannot see much, and I may hurt you by staying here."

"Do not worry! My carcass is solid; it has gone through much more. My shelter is safe, and it will protect you until we find the daylight again. The deep waters are not touched by the big waves. As I promised Yupik, I will take you south."

Feeling reassured, Tali Nohkati made himself comfortable. The plumpness and the reserves of the whale made the place very cozy. Little by little, he grew used to the magical space as well as the harmonious and monotonous sound of the heart.

Atii, who continued navigating within the shallow waters, could feel the warmth of the child inside her. He was her best catch: a catch of tenderness, life and hope. Thus, she gave him plenty to eat. She treated him to shrimp and squid.

Once sated, when Tali Nohkati wanted to take a nap, she would sing. When he wanted to stretch his legs, she would guide him through her womb for a hide-and-seek game.

Tali Nohkati, trying to capture everything happening outside, would frequently question Atii. The whale became his eyes and his only link with the outer world. And that world of Atii was immense.

She would wake him up as soon as dawn broke and lulled him to sleep when the stars appeared. She would tell him of the colors of the sea. While Tali Nohkati thought that the sea was blue, Atii would describe how steadily it changed colors. Beneath the sky, the clouds came and went, the stars shined or faded away, the moon appeared and disappeared. The ocean, a receptacle of lights, captured their reflections. This was how she knew if the wind blew softly or picked up.

Atii told him how the waves were born. First, there is nothing. The water is only a polished mirror, flattened by the winged spirits. The mermaids love admiring themselves in it. But, all of a sudden, as stillness takes over, a subtle movement slowly carries them. The fish, with their multicolored scales, the coral branches and all the sea creatures drift along with the currents. Is it the dance of the Earth? Is it the jolt of its depths?

Atii said that it was a secret. Whatever it was! Tali Nohkati was listening, mesmerized. With the opals forgotten by the Moon, he drew the visions of this other universe on the ribs of the whale. Soon, a fresco adorned the cave which was sheltering his sleep, and his dreams took him to the Outer Limits.

How long did that journey last, an incredible one, at the very least? How to know when the night and the day did not exist anymore?

Tali Nohkati never knew. Only the wonderful words of Atii would guide his voyage.

Atii knew that soon she would be swimming along the Land of the North. To her great regret, Tali Nohkati was going to leave her, almost certainly forever.

She woke him up, announced the news to him and took advantage of their last moments together to lavish some more advice on him.

"Be careful, make sure you do not lower your guard. The shores of this region are long and steep, flanked by black rocks. For all I know, a vast forest spreads a few steps away from the beach, but I have never seen a living soul there. Of course, some birds fly there to build their nest, but no men like you."

Tali Nohkati was listening attentively, knowing nothing of the place where she was going to leave him. And oddly enough, while Atii's heartbeats had been his companion during the entire crossing, it was now his own heartbeat which he could hear.

The time had come to say goodbye. Atii stopped swimming and told Tali Nohkati to come close to her mouth.

"Did you pick up the skin clothes and the stones from the Moon?" the whale asked.

Tali Nohkati, struck by the coolness of the air, nodded.

"Are you ready?" She asked him again, deeply moved.

Tali Nohkati, as moved as she was, nodded again. All of a sudden and without further warning, he was hurled into the sky. With the swift and powerful blow of Atii, he recovered the light. He flew like a bird and found himself landing on a shore of light sand.

Stunned, Tali Nohkati ran his eyes over the surface of the water, looking for the presence of Atii. For a brief moment, he caught a glimpse of her before she disappeared into the depths of the ocean.

Tali Nohkati, getting used to the new scenery, started to pace the beach up and down. He found a few eggs, a few shells. He lit a fire, ate a little. Finally, he found a path and disappeared into the forest.

4 WITH THE WOLVES

The pervading smell of the earth revived the memories of Tali Nohkati, those of a distant time, when fishing and foraging defined life among his people.

Every discovery would equally delight and worry him: the majesty of the trees, the rustling of the leaves, the mystical display of shadows and lights, the singing of the birds, the screeches of the animals or the cracking of the branches.

Having walked most of the day, Tali Nohkati noticed the fading Sun and allowed the lapping of the water to guide him. He soon found himself on the banks of a river where he decided to settle for the night.

He refreshed his body in the cool water, ate what was left of his provisions. Finally, he laid down next to a glowing fire and gazed at the stars which appeared one by one in the sky.

He was listening to the sounds of the night when a familiar yelp startled him. Could it be that Coyote was here? Was it the fatigue playing a trick on him or a malicious dream coming to torment him?

He heard another yelp. Tali Nohkati called for Coyote, since the darkness rendered all search impossible. He called his name as loudly as he could. He called his name again and again. But nobody answered Tali Nohkati, not Coyote or another animal, so he stayed still, suspended in the silence which had suddenly fallen on the deep dark forest.

Then, to push away the threatening shadows of his fears, he rekindled his fire and, piqued, sank deep into sleep.

In the morning, Tali Nohkati awoke. He was gathering the last embers when he saw, on the other bank, a wolf watching him. Careful and to avoid startling the animal, Tali Nohkati decided to not try to run away. Instead, he chose to sit still and wait.

The wolf, intrigued, wanted to know who the intruder was, who had ventured into his territory. He crossed the river and slowly walked towards Tali Nohkati. As he came upon him, he circled and sniffed him, looking deeply into his eyes and said:

"I am not the one you heard last night. My name is Haida. And you, who are you?"

Feeling scared, Tali Nohkati introduced himself and told his story. At the end of his story, the wolf confided in him:

"You were lucky! Does your flesh have no flavor or have my fellow wolves lost their appetite? Still, when I look at you, I can assure you they could easily devour you in one bite! So could I, for a start!"

Then, he added:

"Luck is a rare thing in these lands. I am afraid you will not be able to survive for long alone, unless..."

"Unless?" Tali Nohkati asked, worried.

"Unless you can help us in some way. What are your skills?"

Tali Nohkati hastened to list out all his skills: foraging, fishing, hunting, preparing fish and meat. The latter skill particularly caught the attention of the wolf who then offered:

"I have a large family and the last litter, voracious. If you want, I will make sure my pack accepts you."

Tali Nohkati agreed. He ventured deep into the forest with Haida and asked him:

"If Coyote is not here, would you then know where I could find him?"

But he could not hear the answer. Already, a herd of noisy and mischievous wolf cubs was rushing towards them.

There were five of them. Pasko, Nissoac, Swac, Iwac and Nonoac, five bouncing brothers and sisters, happy to finally be leaving the den that had sheltered them since birth.

The presence of Tali Nohkati by their father's side roused their curiosity. Mimicking the behavior of their elders, they hopped and swirled around the child, nibbling his legs. Haida sent them back to their mother's side, and, as a true pack leader, introduced the newcomer. The females came close to the stranger, sized him up. Having lived for a while with Yupik and Qanuk, Tali Nohkati knew he should not provoke the animals. So, he showed himself to be submissive and docile.

The wolf cubs, viewing him as a playmate, put their trust in him immediately and came back to rub themselves against him.

The day was clear. The softness in the air announced the arrival of spring. Tali Nohkati, pleased by the company, regained confidence. Haida told him:

"Our den could not possibly take you in. You will need a roof."

"Oh! After the hardships of the White Land and Atii's belly, a cave or a hollow tree will do," Tali Nohkati answered.

"Caves are for grizzly bears, the tree branches for the birds and the rivers for the fish. Believe me, each in his own place. It is for the best!"

Tali Nohkati took a moment to think. Drawing from his memories, he recovered the image of a hut where it felt good to sleep. "This is what I must do," he thought. "But, how, how did my father go about it?"

He was absorbed in thought for a while. But the hunger began to gnaw at him. He went to hunt, led by the wolf who knew every corner of the vast forest.

The Land of the North abounded in game, and as soon as he returned from hunting, Tali Nohkati shared his catch, much to the delight of the herd.

Haida, who saw him hunt, knew that his help would be valuable. In spite of his own acute sense of smell and his powerful strength, a prey would occasionally slip out of his paws and endanger the survival of the pack.

Although fresh meat and fish were plentiful, Tali Nohkati made a habit of smoking most of it, so that they would never lack food.

He also foraged for berries and mushrooms. He ventured out, into every path. Pasko, Nissoac, Swac, Iwac and Nonoac leapt at the opportunity and followed him, only too happy to escape from female supervision.

One day, after venturing away from their territory, a thunderstorm took them by surprise. They found shelter in a rocky cavity. The wolf cubs, worried, huddled up against Tali Nohkati. The small flames, which he managed to kindle, provided them with some light and warmth. But the thunderstorm grew more violent, with a deafening thundering and roaring noise. Adding to the rumble of thunder were the howling wind and the bubbling of the flooding river.

Very quickly, the threatening darkness encircled the troop, closing them in.

When night left, all had been destroyed. Under the terrified gaze of the wolf cubs, Tali Nohkati tried eagerly to retrace the steps which had led them there, but the uprooted trees and mudslides squashed all hopes of finding their way.

This was how he unwillingly became the leader of the pack.

Over the next few days, the brothers and sisters did not want to leave their shelter, but Tali Nohkati forced them to resume their journey through the woods.

Many animals had succumbed to the assaults of the thunderstorm. Easy to unearth, the food allowed the pack to regain their strength and overcome this struggle. However, the sustenance was not going to last. The instinct of the inner predators had to be sharpened at once.

The sisters Swac and Iwac proved themselves to be fearless in this game. When they would come back with their first preys, Tali Nohkati congratulated them, stroked them vigorously in encouragement. Thirsting for tenderness and recognition, the young males followed their lead and, little by little, the fear gave way to new life.

They all paid attention to Tali Nohkati's guidance. There was trust, and that trust bound the group together. When some of them went out to hunt, others protected the shelter, and the meals, fairly shared, were a source of immense joy.

The summer slowly drew to a close. Already, autumn set the vast forest ablaze. The red and yellow shades of the foliage reigned supreme.

Tali Nohkati eagerly picked up the last fruit, smoked the wild game, fished the fresh salmons, tanned the dried skins. Sensing the impending arrival of winter, he organized the den so that none of the siblings would suffer again.

Then, one morning, the snow, long-awaited and dreaded, appeared at the far end of the sky. This white screen certainly puzzled the wolf cubs, who were seeing it for the first time. Although reticent at first, they later dashed forward with great delight, dragging Tali Nohkati with them. Ah, these slides, these rolls! How much fun it was!

It was winter, the season of food shortages, of cold and quiet. But they were together, happy to be so. Life was beautiful, very beautiful, especially when Tali Nohkati recounted his journeys to his friends, who could not believe their ears.

Life went on that way, until the arrival of spring.

Freed from the frozen hardships, the time of racing and hunting across the woods had returned. The young wolves were growing up, becoming more and more independent. Tali Nohkati knew they would not resist the call of their destiny much longer.

Swac met him by the river and told him:

"Nissoac, Nonoac and Pasko are going to leave and conquer new territories. My sister Iwac is going to join a pack and, as for me, I am about to pair with the big grey wolf. But what are you going to do?"

"Just like you. Leave, go another way," Tali Nohkati answered, with a lump in his throat.

"How could we ever thank you?" Pasko, who had joined them, asked. "How could we ever forget you? You saved our lives, you gave us new hopes..."

" ... and the strength to fight," Nissoac and Nonoac exclaimed in unison. Their gratitude touched Tali Nohkati. And, since it had to be this way, he walked back, with the wolves in tow, to the rocky cavity that had sheltered them.

The very idea of staying there without them, even for a moment, was unbearable. He packed his belongings promptly.

Before leaving them, he stroked them warmly and hugged them one last time. This is when, as they were parting, Iwac licked his face and told him:

"This morning, I saw the one you called that first night."

"Coyote?!" Tali Nohkati exclaimed.

"He is waiting for you on the other bank."

The Sun at its zenith shone with all its brilliance. The forest exhaled its fragrances, and destiny took each of them away, leading them on their own path.

5 TALI NOHKATI REUNITES WITH COYOTE

"Ah! Tali Nohkati! Tali Nohkati! I am so happy to finally see you again!"
"Coyote! Coyote! I have missed you so much!"
This reunion filled them with joy. Coyote leapt around Tali Nohkati, who roared with laughter.
"You have changed so much!" Coyote said. "But tell me, tell me all about your journey."

Tali Nohkati, unstoppable, recounted his adventures with the bears, the whale and the wolves. Coyote listened to him, filled with wonder. So much courage and boldness commanded his admiration. His heart overflowed with tenderness for the child whose birth he had witnessed.

As they talked, they walked away from the deep forest. The trees, so majestic, allowed more room for light. The immense sky appeared before their eyes, radiant.

At the end of the day, they rested. The emotion had opened their appetites. From his reserves, Tali Nohkati drew some delicacies: smoked fish and meats, a real treat.

In front of the crackling fire, a flood of memories rushed forth: the nights under the stars, the lullabies of the mother, the walks in the plains, the gestures of the father...

"What about you?" Tali Nohkati asked. "What have you been up to?"

"After you left, I wandered, no knowing where to go. I felt your absence in the depths of my soul. But I wanted to live, to see you again and gaze again at the bronze brightness of the Moon. Thus, I started to walk, straight ahead, for days and nights. Little by little, the stars and the sun reappeared in the sky. The dew and the rain quenched my thirst. Suddenly, a vast plain appeared before me. The grass was lush, the food plentiful. Life finally reclaimed its rights, beyond my expectations. One evening, I was about to fall asleep when I saw a fire. Curious, I approached. Crouched in the undergrowth, I then saw a group of men, similar to you."

"How many were they? Where were they coming from?" Tali Nohkati asked, intrigued.

"Being careful to not draw attention, I followed them for several seasons," Coyote said. "The men would hunt together, the women would carry their children on their backs and pick up plants. They would share their catch, each of them having a part and a place within the tribe. None of them suffered. None was forgotten. However, one of them appeared to lead them and to possess great powers. I would often watch him. Respected by all, he would skillfully track down the game, and as evening fell, he would read the path of the stars in the sky."

"How would he do that?" Tali Nohkati questioned.

"I have never known," Coyote admitted. "But, if you met him, he could probably teach it to you and maybe take you in among his own."

"Since you know their territory, could you lead me to them?" Tali Nohkati asked.

"Very well," Coyote said. "At dawn, we will be on our way."

The following day, the forest had completely disappeared and the plain, described by Coyote, unfolded before their eyes.

Undulating and scattered with multicolored flowers, it stretched on endlessly. Tali Nohkati absorbed this new land. Coyote, who had travelled it extensively, knew every inch of it. He could give the child some valuable advice.

They walked all day long, without coming across any living soul. Soon, the night enclosed them and the Moon appeared. She gently landed on the pointed ears of Coyote and exclaimed:

"Tali Nohkati! You have grown so much!"

Moved to see her again, Tali Nohkati showed her the opals that she had forgotten at the time of her visit to the White Land.

"You see, beautiful Moon, I have carried you close to my heart."

This tender gesture moved her to the core. She hugged the boy and confided:

"As Coyote told you, this corner of the earth facilitates encounters. I have seen its paths. There are many. Its high grass dances in the wind..."

Then, she added, with emotion:

"... and its spring rains have the gentleness of the lullabies, which are hummed to the children by the women of the tribe."

As she said this, she kissed Tali Nohkati, stroked the fur of Coyote and softly rose up, disappearing into the night sky.

Many days passed.

Coyote could not quite bring himself to leave Tali Nohkati. Alas, the time had come for him to go. One morning, hiding his sadness, he said to him:

"Aside from the Moon and the preys which we have caught, we have not met anyone. Yet, I can sense that your own people are not too far."

"You are going to leave me once more," Tali Nohkati answered.

"It cannot be otherwise, as you very well know. Nevertheless, I do not want to leave before sharing with you an important detail. It will enable you to recognize the one who leads his own people across the Land of the Plains. An eagle feather adorns his hair."

Trying to hold him back, Tali Nohkati wanted to learn more. But Coyote licked his cheeks and resumed his journey, promising to see him again soon.

The sun at its zenith bathed the plain in golden light. His heart filled with sorrow, Tali Nohkati watched as his friend walked away. He began to think of these men whom he would soon meet, with whom he would share his life. And these thoughts gave him courage.

6 ATSINA, THE BISON

Not far from a river, he found a suitable place that could be used both as a shelter and as a starting point to explore this territory.

Coyote and the Moon had not lied. The land was beautiful and generous, its landscapes magnificent. The radiant summer seemed as if it never wanted to end.

One morning, as he was still dozing, Tali Nohkati felt a wave of warmth on his back. Thinking that Coyote was back, he leapt to his feet. But, what he saw by his side, left him speechless.

A bison was sleeping to his heart's content, snoring enthusiastically. Tali Nohkati could not believe it. He scanned the horizon. But he could not see a herd, which left him puzzled. When the bison woke up, his huge body overwhelmed him, and he took a few steps backward.

"Don't be scared," the animal said to him at once. "I only eat grass."

"Did you get lost? Have the ones of the herd left you behind?" Tali Nohkati asked.

"You are not with them?" the bison asked, in turn, worried.

Facing each other, they sized each other up for a while; the frail Tali Nohkati, no taller than a shrub, and the powerful bison, taller than a block of stone. Finally, the animal broke the silence:

"My name is Atsina. I live alone. This is the fault of the white mark I have between my horns. Because of it, my family and friends rejected me, banished me forever. Thus, I cope on my own. I graze here and there. Luckily, clovers are abundant, the spring water refreshing, my wool all warm for the winter. What about you, what are you doing far from your family?"

In turn, Tali Nohkati told him his adventures. The bison, impressed, listened to him and by the end of the night, they had become the best of friends.

Atsina knew everything: where the soft grass was growing, where the rain was coming from, when the warmest night would come, when the coldest night would come. And the men? Did he know them?

"Of course, I know them," he said proudly. "I have often seen them hunt together."

"And what do they hunt?" Tali Nohkati asked.

"The bison, of course! Our meat, our skin, our fat, it is all good! They would use all of it."

How could Tali Nohkati not have thought of this before! Before his surprised gaze, Atsina added hastily:

"With you, I am at peace. I know that you will eat me only with your eyes."

"I have never eaten a friend," Tali Nohkati confessed. "Plus, you are far too strong and too big for me! My belly could not fit you."

"Your belly alone, no. But imagine many bellies like yours. My meat, carved into thin slices, cooked on the embers, would fill them. You can believe me."

Tali Nohkati believed him unquestioningly, all the more since, for the last few days, his catch had run short. Curious, he asked:

"But, how do they hunt a herd?"

Atsina described to him the terrible confrontation of the animals and the men. The ambushes, the races across the plains, the spears, the wounds, the falls in the gullies, the sweat, the exhaustion, death.

This story reminded Tali Nohkati of his first hunting with Yupik, his expeditions with the wolf cubs, fear and hunger, sometimes so great, sometimes so violent. But he knew it was how things were: one life for one life.

Between the two of them, they made a good team. By Atsina's side, Tali Nohkati would feel protected and would lack nothing. By Tali Nohkati's side, Atsina would find all of the affection he had been desperately craving.

The seasons went by, but no man, no herd would appear on the horizon.

Accustomed to living remotely, Tali Nohkati gathered provisions, amassed some fodder for the winter. A few eagle feathers randomly found during his travels indeed caught his attention but, little by little, his curiosity waned.

The first snowflakes came. In the vast plains, all of a sudden whitened into infinity, silence reigned supreme.

The fire, which Tali Nohkati kept burning, was giving off a cozy warmth inside the shelter. And when the weather was mild, he would go, on the back of the bison, to look for some dead wood or to catch a hare.

At the end of a beautiful day, they saw footprints.

Although the sun had shone through spring and summer times, they had not seen a living soul. And now, a man was venturing alone, in the heart of winter, into this vast land. Where was he going? What was he looking for?

The animal did not express his concerns to Tali Nohkati, but he knew that when a man was walking this way, he was doing it to fetch food for his people. Therefore, it would not take long before he would hunt them out of their shelter.

Atsina could not bear the thought of losing his good companion. As for ending up carved into quarters, it would drive him utterly fierce.

From then on, he made a determined effort to lose the intruder.

Once the danger had passed, life took up its course again. One morning, Atsina told Tali Nohkati:

"The coming night will be very cold. You will have to light a big fire and, if you huddle up to me, you should not suffer from it."

Then, he added:

"I will let you prepare the fire. As for me, I will try to graze on some short grass and will come back home once full."

This is how the day went. Tali Nohkati bustled about, found some small wood and watched out for the animal. All of a sudden, the night took over everything. The bison had not come back. Tali Nohkati, worried, called out to him:

"Atsina! Atsina!"

But, nothing, nothing would come to echo his call.

The icy air stung Tali Nohkati, forcing him to rush back into the shelter. The friendly heat of the flames calmed him down for a while, but his thoughts took him back to Atsina. Where was he? What was he doing? Why was he not back yet?

These questions, left unanswered, increased his anguish, but exhaustion took over, and he sank into a deep sleep.

Dawn found Tali Nohkati, all numb, next to the ashes, still warm from the fire.

Dawn found Tali Nohkati but not Atsina. Atsina, hurt, was far away. The child did not know it yet. Thus, when he saw that the bison was still not back, he set out to find him.

He paced the plain up and down, relentlessly. Finally, the dark mass of Atsina came into sight. Tali Nohkati dashed towards him and saw him lying down on his side, panting.

The animal had slipped and broken a leg. He tried his best to go back to the shelter, but the pain, the exhaustion, and the cold eventually overcame him.

Tali Nohkati tried to relieve Atsina. He covered his aching body, laid his hands on the wound. This eased the bison's pain beyond his hopes. Even so, they both well knew that this accident was going to change their lives drastically.

Sensing that his strength was failing, Atsina confessed:

"The time spent with you gave me a taste of happiness. I was so afraid to lose you, to lose your friendship, that I did all I could to keep us from meeting anyone. Will you forgive me?"

"Of course, I will!" Tali Nohkati answered, sobbing.

"You will now have to resume your journey and meet your fellow men."

As he said so, he confided all he knew about humans to the child.

"But, I am not going to leave without you, I am not going to leave you behind," Tali Nohkati said.

"But who talks of leaving me?" the bison said reassuringly, in a last effort. "You will take me with you. You will eat my meat, and I will give you my strength. You will tan my skin, and I will shelter your nights. With my blood, I will bless the earth which carries you and sees you grow up."

"You are asking me to kill you and eat you. I cannot! I cannot!" the child exclaimed.

"You would rather leave me for the vultures? I beg you, be a man, be strong! I beg you, let me serve you in your life once more."

Tali Nohkati's heart was racing wildly. He could not bring himself to the unbearable. Finally, as he could not take it any longer, he let out a terrible scream and, grabbing his knife, he delivered a deadly blow to his friend. He killed Atsina.

The cold weather persisted.

Tali Nohkati, crushed, remained despondent in his shelter for several days. Then, he went back to the remains of Atsina and dismembered him.

The cold weather persisted, and, one morning, the snow began to melt. The blue of the sky lit up the new day. A softness, long forgotten, filled the space and stroked the child's face.

It was time to go.

Tali Nohkati resumed his journey. He left to meet the men, his fellow men. "With them," he thought, "I will live, breathe, eat, hunt, gaze at the stars and never be alone again."

The Moon saw him from far away, and when she met with Coyote, she told him:

"He was good-looking and proud. Two bison horns adorned his skin clothes. He had a beautiful strap around his head. His steps were confident and appeared to lead him towards some conquest."

"And his heart?" Coyote asked. "How is his heart doing?"

"Sometimes it breaks," the Moon answered. "But it is still beating. It is still beating."

7 ZIA ZIA, THE SNAKE

Tali Nohkati, following the path of the Sun, left the Land of the Plains. In the brightness of a more intense light, other colors caught his eyes. Within this new tormented landscape of rocks and rock faces, the ochre tones fought the red ones, slicing the sky as a blade. Nevertheless, the land, more arid, was still beautiful. A good hunter, Tali Nohkati found food. The water, like the game, was not scarce, and the folds in the rocky walls provided safe shelters. In one of them, he settled down.

At the end of one day, on the path leading to his den, he saw tracks on the ground. Long and thin, they appeared to go and come from nowhere. Tali Nohkati had never seen such tracks before.

Before the sun disappeared below the horizon, he tried to determine their origin. He listened, scanned the surrounding field. To no avail. He did not discover a clue of a suspicious presence. As the night came, Tali Nohkati fell asleep.

The next day, he was woken up by sharp, brief, repetitive noises. Careful, Tali Nohkati only opened his eyes and refrained from moving. The strange noises rang once more. Tali Nohkati sat up and saw, not far from him, a rattlesnake.

In disbelief, they looked at each other for a while. Finally, the animal spoke to Tali Nohkati:

"Ak Chin Chiricahua Cochit Cocopa?"

" ???"

"Chochimi Mohave Seri Toboso Walapai?"

"???"

Disconcerted, the child could only answer:

"Me, Tali Nohkati."

"Ah!" the reptile exclaimed. "Me, Zia Zia!"

And, as he was wriggling around the child, he added:

"I have been watching you for several days, and, well, I wonder what you are doing here, Tali Nohkati all alone. Those who look like you have already left."

Tali Nohkati told him what had happened to him. Zia Zia, attentive, did not miss one word of this story.

"Psiiiiiiiiitt! What an adventure!" the snake whispered, admiring. "Alas, you arrive too late."

The men from here run away from the hot season and move northwards, up to the plains, to hunt.

This hot season, mentioned by the reptile, piqued the curiosity of Tali Nohkati. For he, who only knew of the jolts of the big cold, of the storms and of the summer mildness of the regions that he had walked across, wanted to learn more about it.

"Here, during summer, the fire of the sky reigns supreme. Scorching, it drains, burns, devastates the land. And, when I look at you, with barely any clothes, without scales..."

"Would you advise me to turn back?" Tali Nohkati said, worried.

"You would not make it on time! But do not be afraid!" Zia Zia said. "I know every nook and cranny of this country."

After his dreadful ordeal, the warm friendship of Zia Zia comforted Tali Nohkati. Good company, always joyful, he would constantly whistle, and his advice soon proved to be useful. Day after day, the fire of the sky would become more and more merciless. The blinding sun, mirages, the unbearable heat, the scattered vegetation: the scenery lacked nothing.

In this mineral hell, Zia Zia would guide Tali Nohkati and promptly revealed to him his survival secrets.

One morning, he took him, through steep paths, up to the entrance of a cave. A soothing coolness welcomed them.

Zia Zia, in between rays of sunlight, slithered deep into the cave and invited Tali Nohkati to follow him.

Within a basin of white rocks, a clear wave glistened. Its reflection, bouncing on the faces, brought to life an extraordinary scenery.

Trees danced, does sprang, birds flew, bison ran, fish wriggled, men hunted before the astonished eyes of Tali Nohkati.

On another part of the basin, extraordinary faces came to life. Half men, half beasts, they seemed to watch him, their eyes following him.

Tali Nohkati inched closer to the paintings, touched them. The perfection of the lines and the beauty of the colors captivated him.

"Was this the origin of the world? Was he dreaming or was he under a spell?" He wondered, bewildered.

All of a sudden, a handprint caught his attention. Zia Zia told him the story of these paintings. The story of the men who had made them.

Tali Nohkati listened to him, moved. Inching closer, he placed his hand upon the one which was drawn on the stone. It made his heart beat faster, and he remembered.

He remembered his mother's hand caressing his cheeks. He remembered his father's hand laying on his shoulder.

And, in the absolute silence of the cave, tears slipped down his face, down into the clear water.

Back on the path that brought them to the den, Tali Nohkati, still captivated by what he had just discovered, asked Zia Zia:

"Were you here at the beginning of the world?"

"No, I was born afterward. Yet, its first jolts resounded deep within me. Ah! In a deafening racket, the crust of the earth rose up, collapsed, rose up again. From the bowels of the earth streams of lava and all the promises of this wonderful life adventure sprung out."

Tali Nohkati would never grow tired of listening to Zia Zia, who would eagerly go on:

"The fruit of Coyote's and the Moon's wearing labor, this wonderful adventure was unfolding in indescribable chaos. This could not last! Thus..."

"Thus?" Tali Nohkati asked.

Zia Zia slithered on the ground more and more eagerly. With his supple body perfectly shaped into a circle shining sparkling rays, he explained:

"Since then, the days follow the nights which follow the days. From north to south, from east to west, birds fly in the sky, fish swim in the water, the sun shines from morning to night, stars sparkle from night to morning. Since then, rivers flow into the sea, mountains rise up to the firmament, seasons come and go..."

"And my fellow men, and me?" Tali Nohkati asked, carried away by the witty eloquence of the snake.

"In those days, at the beginning of time, you did not exist yet." Zia Zia said. "Your spirits came across the universe only much later, much later."

"When?" Tali Nohkati wanted to know.

"When Coyote, with his four paws, kneaded the clay vigorously. Only at this moment did you and your fellow men appeared on the green banks of a beautiful river."

This unexpected revelation about his birth suddenly brought Tali Nohkati back to the aridity of the desert.

He took a handful of sand, which slipped through his fingers, as the first years of his young life had. Then, each grain was scattered by the wind to melt into the light.

Days followed nights which followed days. Tali Nohkati and Zia Zia got along well. Their bond alleviated the harshness of the weather. As for the teachings lavished by the reptile, they enabled the child to gain even more independence and increased his stamina.

Feed oneself when food is scarce. Bury oneself in the ground when there is no shade to escape from the burning sun. Wait for darkness to go and hunt. Only under these conditions could they survive. Zia Zia did not want to leave anything to chance alone. Thus, he shared advice on everything that he knew.

Zia Zia added one bit of knowledge which would particularly captivate Tali Nohkati. In the evening, the reptile taught him the basis of the languages spoken by the men. One syllable at the time, he would pronounce the names needed to understand each other. After him, Tali Nohkati would repeat the names of the tribes: Ak Chin Chiricahua, Caniba Tolowa, Chochimi Cocopa, Kittitas Kwalhioqua, Arapaho Talio, Luceros Navajos, Piro Pueblos Taos, Tohono Toboso, Pima Arizona, Karankawa Suma, Twana Bella Bella, Haida Kalapuya, Nipissing Quiripi, Panamint Unami, Missouri Biloxi, Saponi Pikuni.

And, at night, they would repeat these strange words together, singing at the top of their voice under the great arch of the stars.

One morning, Tali Nohkati noted that the hot season would never end.

"You are right," Zia Zia answered. The hot season is endless. And, quite subdued, he added:

"It will never end... your fellow men will not come back."

Surprised, Tali Nohkati looked at him. Zia Zia sighed and admitted:

"I did not know how or when to tell you."

"But, then, what did I see in the cave?" Tali Nohkati asked.

"The memory of a happy time. The one preceding the incandescent blast. This blast swept everything in its path. Nothing could stop the deadly strikes of lightning and the frantic race of flames. Few were those who survived this disaster."

This story unsettled Tali Nohkati. Would he have come back unknowingly to his ancestors' soil? But his train of thoughts was interrupted. Zia Zia, his voice filled with emotion, continued his story:

"I had found shelter in the folds of a mountain. When I came back to the light, the very landscape which we are admiring today was revealed before my eyes. Since then, loneliness, like a curse, has been my only companion. Therefore, when I saw you, I was overjoyed. I did my best for you not to fear me."

"And what would I have had to fear?" Tali Nohkati asked.

"My deadly bite! That was the only thing men would see in me. But you, who are going to leave soon, you tell them that I am more than a creature with a deadly bite."

"I will tell them the truth," Tali Nohkati said. "I will tell them of all you have taught me, all the life lessons that you have given me. I will tell them that I know of more deadly bites, those of the cold, hunger, fear and absence."

"Ah! Tali Nohkati, Tali Nohkati! I am going to miss you so much. But do not wait, do not wait anymore! You need to meet with your fellow men, you need to live with them."

Finally, Zia Zia fell silent. His sorrow was too great. He curled up on Tali Nohkati's lap and embraced the last moments that they were going to spend together.

The time came to set forth. Zia Zia told the child:

"Here are some turquoises which come from the depths of the earth. I give them to you to protect you during your long journey."

Tali Nohkati gazed at them, filled with wonder. In his turn, he removed the opals from the Moon, which he was wearing against his heart, to give them to the reptile.

At this moment, the reptile took the opals of fire and the turquoises.

Before the astonished gaze of the child, he assembled the stones, alternating the gold and blue reflections, thus sealing on the marriage of the sky and earth. The jewelry was beautiful. Tali Nohkati did not dare touch it.

"You can take it," Zia Zia said. "It is yours. Atsina's horns will symbolize your strength and this necklace, your wisdom."

The child carefully put it away and said goodbye to Zia Zia one last time.

Finally, he started down the path. The reptile followed his first steps. Then, he left him. What was the point?

The snake slithered about for several days. He slithered about for several nights, looking back from time to time. The figure of Tali Nohkati faded away, and Zia Zia returned to the folds of the old mountain which had sheltered him the day of the great cataclysm.

8 NI-KI-TIJA, NI-GA-TIJA

Following Zia Zia's wise advice, Tali Nohkati travelled northwards.

Day after day, the heat became less intense. The burnt ochre of the rocky walls made way for the vibrant green of the lush meadows. The water flowed down in sparkling rivulets. The treetops quivered in the soft breeze. Birds sang.

The catches of Tali Nohkati were as tasty as the game and the berries plentiful. In view of this luxury, the aridity of the desert seemed only a dream.

In spite of the reptile's absence, which saddened him, he was happy to resume his journey.

In the evening, by the glow of a good fire, memories crowded around him, forming an invisible circle. He felt as though he were seeing his former companions again.

What had become of them? Had time battered them up or spared them? Would he meet them again at a turn on a beach, a hill, a forest or a glacier?

Was Atsina's strength coursing through his veins? Was his good friend Zia Zia still sleeping sheltered from a rock, as they would together?

What had happened to Coyote since he last saw him? What was the Moon doing when he could not see her in the sky?

These thoughts swirled around as he sat before the flames, taking him into the corners of his memory, where cruel and joyful images from his past danced.

At dawn, Tali Nohkati resumed his journey without noticing the presence of Coyote.

Coyote was following the child whom he had seen born. He could not bear to see him suffer anymore.

"Is this the way that men have to live?" The Moon had asked him, one evening, angry. "This is not what we had in mind."

"No, this is not what we had in mind!" Coyote had answered. "But do not worry. From a good distance, I will be watching his steps. He will not lack anything."

And Tali Nohkati advanced through the long grass, on the hillsides. When his steps led him to a plateau, he would gaze at the horizon and say:

"How big this is! How beautiful!"

He had learned so much that he now knew when the wind would blow, when the rain would fall. And he loved it when the wind and the rain would wash his face. He loved it when the earth would exhale its floral and fruity scents, its scents of life.

As the plain he walked on was bathed in the last light of the day, Tali Nohkati laid down on the ground, under the shelter of a tree.

The coolness soothed his body, which ached from the long walk. Lulled by his heartbeat, he dozed off.

Little by little, his heartbeat grew more intense until it felt like the heartbeat of the earth was answering his.

What a strange feeling! Had he gone back into the body of Atii the whale? Had he gone back into his mother's body? He could not tell. This night, his eyes, shut by his dreams, could not perceive the brightness of the stars anymore.

That very night, Coyote left Tali Nohkati.

He had left with the sound of the drums. He had left because a man had come near the child whom he had seen born.

But Tali Nohkati was sleeping soundly and did not know it yet.

-PART TWO-

We know it, the Earth does not belong to man.
Man belongs to Earth.
We know it, all things are linked.
Whatever happens to the Earth happens to the sons of the Earth.
Man did not weave the web of life.
He is merely a strand in it.
Whatever he does to the web, he does to himself.

Seattle, Suquamish Indian Chief

9 RAKENIKA

After a journey which had led him from the White Land to the Land of the Red Earth, Tali Nohkati, who went off in search of his fellow men, laid down one evening, under the shelter of a tree.

The coolness of the ground soothed his body, which ached from the walk, and, lulled by his heartbeat, he sank into sleep.

The man who found him leaned over him. An eagle feather adorned his hair. He made sure that the child was not hurt and that no one else was lurking nearby.

This presence, not far from his camp, piqued his curiosity.

Seeing that the child was not waking up, he scooped him up and carried him to his fellows. They all came close to see the stranger. Then, the man laid him down in his tepee.

A soft light radiated around the fire. As to not scare him, the man and the woman watched him silently.

If the skin, the bison horns and the turquoises were familiar to them, the facial features and the fiery opals, on the other hand, aroused their curiosity and made them wonder.

Whilst keeping their eyes on the child, they whispered:

"What is he doing alone at night? Did he get lost? Was he abandoned? Where is he coming from? Where is his tribe?"

But the night went by, holding Tali Nohkati in the depths of his dreams, without offering an answer.

Rakenika, the man who had found him, and Gaho, his wife, watched over him until dawn.

At sunrise, the man went out to check some traps and the woman to fetch the water.

Iktomi, the spider, chose that very moment to glide along her silk thread down to Tali Nohkati. Hanging over his head, she blew on his forehead to wake him up.

As he opened his eyes, Tali Nohkati was surprised to not see the branches above his head.

"Is this the web you have spun during the night?" he asked the spider.

Iktomi made him understand, through the power of signs, that four lives would not be enough.

"But then, where did you take me while I was sleeping?" Tali Nohkati asked.

"   ... (It is rather me who found you here!)"

"Here, where is it?" Tali Nohkati wanted to know.

"   ... (Here is the land of your fellow men)"

Tali Nohkati could not believe it. Finally! Finally, he had arrived!

"Where are they?"

Iktomi pushed the canvas of the tepee, and Tali Nohkati leaped up and darted outside. The sky was clear. Around a fire, where a few women bustled about, several tepees formed a circle.

Some children played tag, running after each other.

Suddenly, all gazes fell on him. The smile on the face of Tali Nohkati was inviting and they approached, as did the couple who had taken him in.

In a tumult, Tali Nohkati was bombarded with questions. They all wanted to know who he was. Where he was coming from.

Recognizing the words Zia Zia, the rattlesnake, had taught him, Tali Nohkati happily introduced himself. The women brought him food and drink. The children dragged him to play with them at once.

Finally, as the day began to die down, the whole tribe gathered around the fire. And, sitting next to Rakenika, the man who had found him, Tali Nohkati told them about his great journey.

For several evenings, the stories of Tali Nohkati captivated the members of the tribe: Yupik and her bear-cub, the ice field and the high ice walls, the bowels of Atii the whale, the wolf- cubs in the deep forest, the vast plains with Atsina, the scorching desert with Zia Zia.

At the end of this story, Rakenika spoke:

"Tali Nohkati! Tali Nohkati! All the paths that you have followed could never be guessed from your name. Where does it come from? Who gave it to you?"

"Alas!" the child answered. "My memory does not serve me well. From a distant past, I can only recall a few shadows: my father's hand on my shoulder, my mother's smile. But above all, a burning blast, a blast which takes them from me and leaves me alone, so alone. And if..."

But Tali Nohkati did not have enough time to finish his sentence. Rakenika, seeing his tears well up as he evoked his past, stood up and announced:

"Alone, you are not anymore. Since your journey under the sun and the stars has brought you here, we adopt you. With time and through your actions, you will become one of us."

Turning towards the other members, he added:

"If one of you objects, then throw a handful of soil into the fire."

No one threw soil into the flames.

As a token of recognition, the men, the women and the children approached Tali Nohkati and laid their hands on his heart.

That evening, Rakenika did not mention the fiery opals.

That evening, he let Tali Nohkati be born a second time.

And, like at the beginning, the round Moon shone high in the sky and Coyote sang in the night.

10 NITIS, TAKODA AND TALI NOHKATI

The days following his adoption gave Tali Nohkati a chance to make thousands of new discoveries.

The assembly of a tepee, the cooking of a meal, the making of a piece of clothing or of a hairdo, everything amazed him. It was all delightful to him.

With patience, each member taught him how to do each thing. And Tali Nohkati diligently learned to reproduce the gestures that he sensed were essential to the life of the group.

He became friends with Nitis and Takoda, two mischievous and intrepid boys. Very soon, they were inseparable.

They would always be together, playing and chasing each other, running until out of breath. Groves, rivers, hills, their playground had no boundaries.

For Tali Nohkati, they would simulate hunting scenes, catch fish, crayfish.

For his new friends, fascinated by the stories that he had told, Tali Nohkati would mimic every act and gesture of his adventures.

In these endless spaces, with his fellow men, he was happy. Days passed by, and he felt braver, taller. Inwardly, he was saying it to the Moon and Coyote.

Taller, he was most certainly. Rakenika and Gaho knew it well.

As guardians of the law and the customs, they also knew that the end of childhood had come for the one whom, from then on, they were calling their son, as well as for his two companions.

The time for initiation had come. Tomorrow, these young buds would blossom and shed their age as animals their skin.

At dawn, the young boys gathered together. Under the lead of

Rakenika, they walked away from the camp.

Soon, the familiar landscape disappeared.

Iktomi, the spider, had found shelter behind Tali Nohkati's ear. Guardian of his dreams and nights, she had also adopted him. Sensing his distress, she tapped on the crook of his neck:

"   . (Do not worry. I am here.)"

"Is that the way it is for all men?" Tali Nohkati asked.

"   . (It is that way! You very well know it; it is good to learn in order to live.)"

With the Sun at its zenith, they reached the edge of a clearing. Several men of the tribe welcomed them and handed out a bag with a few supplies to each of them.

The young boys took advantage of this moment of rest to come together.

"I am anxious to know what we are going to do," Nitis and Takoda let out with one voice.

"What a mystery!" Tali Nohkati said in turn.

"From what I know," Takoda confided. "We will soon be allowed to take part in the big hunts."

"We will be allowed to marry and to fight," Nitis added.

But Rakenika and the men were already forming groups. The three friends were not separated and the first lesson started.

They might have known how to set traps and track down small game animals, but hunting the bison or chasing the enemy required other skills.

Shooting bows, using a knife, running for several days, waiting patiently and quietly without moving, regardless of weather and place. But also, invoking the spirits, singing to make the rain fall, learning to endure and not suffer. This was what the tribe would expect from them. Having been exposed already to the most extreme conditions in the past, Tali Nohkati quickly mastered the hunting exercises and took the lead.

Foremost, they were fascinated by the handling of the bow, the knife and the spear. Placed in expert hands, the power of these weapons would become so immense that they felt invincible. Nitis, Takoda and Tali

Nohkati learned how to make them, how to strike fast and strong.

What animal could resist their impact? Which enemy would dare confront them?

But that enemy, if he is not the wild animal, if he is not the river overflowing its banks, if he is not the wind amassing clouds, then who is he? Where does he come from?

Rakenika told them:

"The enemy is the one you do not expect. His hands muffle his victims' screams and, with fatal blows, he can crush life and depart souls."

Then, he added:

"The most dangerous and ruthless enemy looks like you. You must fight him with strength and bravery."

At once, feeling as if they had been entrusted with an important mission, the teenagers raised their heads proudly, ready to fight. But Tali Nohkati did not understand. Who on earth would want to fight him? And why?

Suddenly, he remembered the bear which was lurking around Yupik the she-bear, to devour Qanuk, her cub. He remembered his torn white fur. This vision filled him with dread, and he felt deep within the rage that he would use today to defend the cub.

Days passed by, each bringing their share of knowledge. The rigors of the trainings showed on their tired faces. However, none of them complained, too proud to dutifully accomplish this rite of passage.

At dusk, Rakenika, gathering the young men, turned towards the setting sun. There, he would tell them of the mountains, the trees, and the Sun. He would tell them of the world and of the Great Spirit.

The initiation was coming to an end, but the teenagers had to carry out a final test. Separated from one another, they had to find a place to stay for four days and four nights. Four days and four nights of solitude during which, under the watchful eyes of Rakenika and of the elders, they would be forced to stay without moving, without talking, without eating and without drinking.

Although the search for food had taught Tali Nohkati how to tolerate hunger and thirst, he had never had to face the overwhelming visions that gradually came over him.

Not succumbing to fear, the strangeness and weakness due to the long fast made him shiver. Then, realizing that any resistance would be in vain, he let it go.

It was like a succession of mysterious dreams, some of which would stay indelibly printed on his memory.

The blue of his turquoises, similar to rivers, flowed out from the creases on his palms and ran into the ocean in majestic sprays.

At the bottom of a bison's horn, settled gold and silver nuggets.

At the top of a mountain, multicolored feathers rose, and a fiery animal, which nobody knew about, carried them across the world.

The day after his last night, Rakenika shook Tali Nohkati out of his stupor. He gave him some fruit and some bread. Then, meeting one another, they walked back toward the camp. Upon their return, the women and children joyfully and proudly welcomed these new men who would guide and protect them.

In the evening, sitting around the crackling fire and keeping with tradition, nobody told of what they had lived through. But there was rejoicing. Dressed in their finest clothes, they danced and sang to show the Great Spirit that they loved life.

Tali Nohkati, happy, danced and sang along with them, under the full Moon. He danced and sang to show Coyote that, from now on, he was a man among men.

11 The Great Hunt

Tali Nohkati was always carrying the opals and the turquoises over his heart. Intrigued, Rakenika wondered: Are those stones sacred? Do they have a supernatural power? Are they all that he has left from his family and friends?

Respectful of the silence from the one who was, as of now, his son, he did not ask any question. He only thought that one night, one night under the stars, the time to speak would come.

His mind began to wander.

Recently, he could feel the heartbeat of the earth. First imperceptibly, the grass and the tree branches quivered, as if caressed by a summer breeze. Then, he detected the faraway echo of the bison's progression.

The great hunt was about to begin.

Buoyed by this exceptional event, the men gathered together to sharpen their weapons. The women and children assembled the utensils necessary for the preparation of the meat and for the tanning of the skins.

Nothing would be lost. Nothing would be thrown away.

The bison gave everything the men needed and, as he looked at them, Tali Nohkati remembered Atsina's words.

Finally, led by Rakenika, the tribe set off and soon, in the clear dawn of a new day, the whole large herd came into view.

Tali Nohkati had never seen anything like it.

Before his astonished eyes, the bison, which had come to fertile pastures, gathered together in the deep heart of the valley.

But how would they, his companions and himself, reach them? Will the bows be enough? What would they do if the animals started to charge?

Rakenika reassured Tali Nohkati and, while the women were setting up the campsite, he invited the best hunters of the tribe and the young initiates to follow him.

Faced with these wild animals, nothing should be left to chance. Wounds were not rare, and no unnecessary risk should be taken. Hence, they decided together on the strategy to adopt and on the role each of them was to play.

They walked away from the tepees and started to inch closer. The fantastic mass of the herd gradually revealed itself.

Apprehension and fear swept over the minds, but, in the end, the desire to confront the animals overcame the last shred of resistance.

As the females and their offspring spared, the men encircled some males standing apart. They screamed and succeeded in moving them away, leading them towards a narrower pass. This pass, which Rakenika knew well, was bordered by high walls, on which the men could stand. Thus protected, they could reach the animals securely and without too much risk.

Nitis, Takoda and Tali Nohkati, toughened by what had been taught to them, displayed great bravery. They shot their arrows with dexterity and skill, killing several bison at one go. In spite of the painful memory of the deadly blow that he had delivered to Atsina, Tali Nohkati, who had faced the dangers and the difficult wait of the solitary hunter, discovered the exaltation and the competition that came from hunting together.

For each killed animal, he knew Rakenika and Gaho would be proud of him. He knew that the valiant Nitis and Takoda would be his life-long friends. And this could not make him happier.

Encouraged by their early successes, the three young friends got carried away. And they underestimated the strength and the intelligence of their preys.

Willing to protect the females and their offspring, the males, aware of the human presence, got nervous. They surrounded the herd on all sides, making it more and more difficult to attack.

In a tactful and bold manner, Rakenika succeeded in breaking one front and opening a breach through which they could approach.

Without losing sight of his every move, Tali Nohkati followed him. All of a sudden, the animals, seeing they were assailed from every direction, furiously pounded at the ground and dashed towards the hunters.

The bison ran at top speed. The ground shook. The noise of their race covered the screams of the men.

As he ran away with the others, Tali Nohkati stumbled and fell. He tried to resume his run. Alas, his companions had already left him, and a ferocious herd surrounded him.

His heart beat wildly. Fear took hold of him, swept over him. Scared, he was still able to pull himself together, but what could he do? Even armed with his bow and his knife, he could never kill so many animals by himself.

This truth made his blood run cold. His mind became a jumble of confusing dark thoughts.

Was it Atsina's spirit manifesting itself? Was it his bravery abandoning him?

The bison were encircling him, sniffing him. In this way, they made him their prisoner. Suddenly, an absolute silence filled in the space. Time, as if suspended, had buried all noises and Tali Nohkati, trapped, found himself alone between the sky and earth.

Suddenly, nothing would connect him anymore to his fellow men. Vanished, the words, the gazes and the laughs. Bygone, the howl of Coyote and the bronze glow of the opals. Under the crescent of the Moon, so pale at this time of the day, he knew only one thing: here was the end of his journey. It was here and now that he was going to die.

When he could not see Tali Nohkati anymore, Rakenika worried.

As the brown mass of the herd blocked the horizon, it all became clear. Alone, Tali Nohkati found himself at great risk.

Without missing a beat, Rakenika asked the hunters to give him cover while he defied and chased the animals away.

In the Land of the Plains, his courage was legendary and, in spite of the risks, the men of the tribe complied without protest.

Rakenika walked around the herd that encircled Tali Nohkati.

Lying low in the tall grass, facing the wind, he inched closer to a female and her offspring in order to call the attention of the males.

The diversion was slowly taking place, and Rakenika looked for Tali Nohkati in the most hidden folds of the ground.

He finally found him. Under the muzzle of an enormous bison, he appeared to have lost consciousness.

Taming his fears, Rakenika crawled closer. He inched so close that he could look deeply into the animal's eyes. He stood still, holding his breath.

Proud, the formidable bison seemed to be watching over his prey.

For a long time, the man and the animal stayed this way, facing each other.

Rakenika knew that, at the slightest move, he would gore the frail body of Tali Nohkati.

Thus, he decided to wait.

But he also knew, from his heartbeat, that he was not afraid. He knew that patience often is the best resistance, that love is stronger than slyness. He knew he would save the son whom Providence had given to him.

And Providence echoed his certitude. At nightfall, the bison walked away.

Tenderly, Rakenika picked Tali Nohkati in his arms and took him back to his fellow men. Back at the campsite, Gaho lavished the best care on her protégé and, in front of the evening fire, the hunters told of their chief's exploit.

"If death is such, then it must be sweet," Coyote said to himself as he watched Tali Nohkati. Quietly, he had slipped into the tepee. He could hear the regular breathing of the child whom he had seen born and was talking to him as if he were awake:

"Fortunately, you are not dead, you are only asleep. Gaho's remedies have soothed you." Coyote placed his muzzle next to Tali Nohkati's face and whispered:

"We nearly lost you. But your heart is beating and blood is running through your veins. Tonight, I will go and say it to the Moon. We were so scared!"

Coyote stood up and, after placing a fiery opal on Tali Nohkati's forehead, he said before leaving:

"She wanted me to give this to you. So that you keep it against your heart."

In the middle of the day, while Tali Nohkati still slept, Rakenika saw the stone.

As it lit up the sides of the tent, its magnificent glow fascinated him. Intrigued, he wondered which spirit was looking after his son.

But when Tali Nohkati opened his eyes, he gave him the stone without saying a word. He smiled at the young man who had recovered his strength, the young man whom he would take hunting again, who would share his life again.

The father and son hugged each other, so happy to not have been separated by fate.

At once, Rakenika took Tali Nohkati to the other members of the tribe. There was so much to do!

To dismember, tan the skins, smoke the meat, make new weapons and hunt the small game. Before winter, there was plenty of work to do.

But also to pick up the berries, the fruit, harvest the three sisters- the beans, the corn and the squash- and play, running around with Nitis and Takoda.

On the generous land, the catches were plenty, the food reserve was full, children had been born, and tomorrow, there would be a great feast.

12 ONE NIGHT UNDER THE STARS

Fall had come back with its procession of rains, the winter with its veils of mist.

As did Zia-Zia the snake, Iktomi the spider had assembled the fiery opal to the gold and azure necklace. The marriage, thus sealed, of the Sky and Earth was resting again on Tali Nohkati's chest.

Rakenika was seeing him grow and he decided that the time to speak had come. Thus, he asked him to gather some supplies and to follow him.

Little by little, the paths took them away from the tribe.

The whiteness of the landscapes through which they walked sparkled under the Sun. Here and there, some prints would give away the presence of stags, lynxes and ermines.

The tree branches bowed down under the weight of snow. Some birds fluttered among the trees, in search of a few seeds or small worms.

Held captive in the ice, the impetuous mountain streams no longer flowed.

Save for the sound of snow crunching under their steps and for their voices, the sleeping land was very quiet.

After several days of walking, mountains loomed on the horizon. Tali Nohkati had never before seen such large ones. Finally, they arrived and took shelter in the fold of the rock.

Tali Nohkati thought: "This place must be sacred. This mountain must hold a secret which Rakenika is the only one to know."

But while the rocks of the desert were inhabited by lush fauna, exuberant flora and strange faces, these were dark and grey, bare and cold to the touch.

Yet, Rakenika seemed at ease here. Soon, magnificent flames started to flicker as he lit a fire. The kind warmth spread around and, as the day ended, the first star appeared.

This night, for which Rakenika had been waiting a long time, had come. And seemingly fulfilling his wish, it was of exceptional beauty.

A blue-shaded glow wreathed the mountains and the undergrowth. Within the infinite sky, the Pleiades twinkled. The shining golden bronze disc of the Moon cast its silky beams. Filled with wonder, Tali Nohkati remembered the White Land that he had crossed long ago, and he could not take his eyes off the satellite.

Rakenika came close to him:

"Do you know that first came the Moon in the sky, that she wanted to reign supreme? For our life, the Morning Star, endowed with great powers, went to war against her. Helped by the other stars and the Sun, she triumphed, and there was the first day, the first night."

As Tali Nohkati felt the fiery opals which the Moon had given to him, their softness, their warmth, the revelation unsettled him.

But under the stone arches, he listened without showing any emotion. And Rakenika, the storyteller, added:

"The Morning Star, you will honor. The other stars, you will know them, for they are the ones who trace the path for men on earth."

He took out a big roll of skin out of a wooden case. The reading of the drawings revealed the constellations. Here, the Big Dipper, there, the Pole Star, forming an eternal round.

This map spread on the floor was like a mirror. It was so accurate that the sky was reflected on it.

Tali Nohkati was puzzled. His gaze was going from the firmament to the stars drawn on the parchment. He wanted to know, he wanted to understand.

In front of the dancing flames, Rakenika told him how the Great Raven had concealed the Sun; why the Hare had asked for the daylight; why the Fox wanted the night to never end.

All ears, Tali Nohkati did not miss one word of this fantastic story. And Coyote, who was not very far away, also heard it.

"I have walked under the sky, unaware," Tali Nohkati said. "But what could I see when my belly was complaining of hunger with Yupik on the icefield, when the entrails of Atii the whale helped me as a shelter, when the wolves' den was hidden away in the heart of the forest? What could I observe when the dazzling Sun forced us, Zia Zia the snake and myself, to look for the shade of the caves, or when I cried for killing Atsina the bison?"

"You walked under the sky, innocent," Rakenika answered. "And you have learned so much! When they do not break you, the cold and the blood make you braver. When they do not doom, hunger and fear teach better than the wise man."

Tali Nohkati poked the flames, resuming their dance, his necklace exposed by the low neckline of his clothing. The precious sparkle radiating from it stunned Rakenika, who asked:

"Is that all you have left from your family and friends?"

Tali Nohkati ran his fingers over the stones and said:

"I have many words to tell my journey but very few to talk about me. But I often dream. Let me tell you what I see. There is a river. It flows peacefully. I am next to my father. He is fishing. His catches are drying in the Sun. Sometimes, my mother carries me on her hips. She is walking. The grass is tall. I can feel it on my legs. She is picking up red berries. The fruit is tasty. The juice runs out and colors my cheeks. Sometimes, my father sits by the water. He brushes stones one against the other. Some, very thin, cut well. Some are round and smooth. They roll with the current or on the bank."

Tali Nohkati kept silent for a while and added:

"The stones of my necklace may come from there. My father may have shaped them for my mother. Sometimes, in my dream, I can hear her. She laughs, she calls me or rocks me. My head is resting on her milk filled breast. She is beautiful."

This vision brought back memories in Rakenika's heart. Moved, he whispered:

"Gaho also had soft and heavy breasts. Gaho also laughed until the Spirit of Earth took away our first newborn."

Taking Tali Nohkati in his arms, he added:

"But today, Gaho and I, we smile again since the Spirit of Earth sent you to us."

Dawn found them next to the ashes, still warm, a little tired but eating heartily.

Then, they headed back.

Save for the snow crunching under their steps and for their voices, the sleeping land was quiet.

The tree branches bowed down under the weight of snow. Some birds fluttered among the trees, in search of a few seeds or small worms.

Being held captive in the ice, the impetuous mountain streams no longer flowed.

Little by little, they approached the tribe.

Around them, the diaphanous nacre of the landscapes they crossed sparkled in the light.

Here and there, some prints gave away the presence of does, wild cats and one coyote.

For a moment, Tali Nohkati looked around for him. But Coyote was not there anymore.

At daybreak, Coyote had climbed to the top of the high mountain and, in his sharp-fanged mouth, the Morning Star, the glorious, the warrior, was held prisoner.

13 THE RAID

In the half-light, Iktomi the spider stood guard.

All her senses awake, she felt a jerk move the threads of her web. Curious, she hurtled down the sides of the tepee.

Dawn was unsettled, still.

Yet, the frail body of Iktomi shook and muffled rumbles coming from the entrails of the Earth made her downy skin bristle.

Alerted, she rushed towards Tali Nohkati. Tapping his face with all her legs, she tried to wake him up. To no avail. He swept the pest away with the back of his hand.

She turned back, stormed the faces of Rakenika and Gaho. They also pushed her away. While sleep was keeping the men in its abyss, the rumbles approached.

Alas, Iktomi the spider did not know how to talk to men. Iktomi, the silent one, could only signal to them.

But often, words and signs cannot do anything for men. Iktomi knew it too well. Helpless, she saw a shadow loom on the horizon. Like a threatening cloud, this shadow moved forward, as if blown by the wind.

The hammered ground panted under the attacks of an unknown force. Suddenly, horsemen, beside themselves with violence and rage, swooped down on the tribe.

Faster than lightning, these warriors wreaked havoc.

Painted faces, piercing eyes, armed with knives, axes and torches, they dashed forward with loud cries, setting fire to the campsite, forcing the tribe members to run away.

Taking advantage of fear and panic, they struck without respite.

Caught off-guard, Rakenika and those who had not been struck yet tried as hard as they could to counter the wild horde. Tali Nohkati, along with Nitis and Takoda, were among them. On their horses, the strangers dominated their victims and inflicted wounds and suffering. Managing to throw some of them off balance, Tali Nohkati and his friends were caught in this diabolical storm and fought to eliminate them. The fighting was of unequal and unparalleled brutality. Nothing could stop the assailants. Around them, everything was falling to pieces. The women, the children, helpless, were dying. The food, the skins, everything was ransacked, everything was pillaged. And what could not be taken was destroyed.

Soon, the clearing which had welcomed the tribe was nothing but a vast battlefield.

In the paleness of winter, the trampled bodies disappeared into the ground. The tepees burned, like stakes; the moans of the wounded rose on the icy air.

Tali Nohkati, redoubling his efforts and his courage, did not succeed in saving Takoda, who succumbed by his side. Overwhelmed with horror and disgust, he started to run, managing to pull himself up on the horse of the one who was leading the warriors. In a swift movement, he grabbed him, made him fall. A merciless fight started between the two. The enemy, relentless, delivered blows and brutalities to Tali Nohkati. But Tali Nohkati, driven by rage and despair, did not surrender.

In the paleness of winter, he stood up. Grabbing the hair of his enemy with one firm hand, he dealt him a final blow. And, with a scream which tore apart the black veil on his heart, he brandished the scalp of his enemy.

It was like thunder. The sight of this bloody trophy defeated the fearsome army. Deprived of their chief, the horsemen retreated and disappeared into the horizon, like a threatening cloud blown away by the wind.

Each and all held their breath, ready to resume the fight if the enemy came back.

Silence fell on the battlefield. Rakenika counted his living and his dead. Tali Nohkati helped him in this macabre task.

Gaho and the women who had survived the massacre took care of the wounded. Bandaging, relieving, calming, it had to be done fast, before grief came in its turn, cutting into the remaining strength.

The surviving men gathered what was left of the meat and the skins. Soon enough, they would have to go and hunt again to feed their family. They would have to go back to shelter their lives.

The cold was biting the day and the souls. Nitis lit up a big fire. Those who lived gathered, their sorrow mixed with their breath to bury and honor the deceased. Under the bison skin that he had thrown on his shoulders, Tali Nohkati rocked a surviving infant. Soothed, he babbled and smiled. His eyes, sparkling with promise, searched for the eyes of Tali Nohkati who kissed his forehead and cheeks. The child clung to the chest of this giant, played with the fiery opals and the turquoises. In the torn hearts, their gentle ringing resounded strangely.

Tali Nohkati wanted to take the child's hands to warm them up more. But the sight of the blood stains on his own hands held him back.

He entrusted Gaho to take good care of the infant and looked at his hands, reddened with the blood of his victims, the blood of men.

But who were these men and where did they come from?

"I will tell you," Rakenika whispered, guessing his thoughts. "I will tell you when pain does not stifle me anymore."

All of a sudden, snow started to fall intermittently, slowly erasing all traces of the carnage. Rakenika decided to leave for the foothills of the high mountains. The caves, numerous in this remote area, would shelter them until the end of winter.

Soon, they were followed by the horses of the riders who were killed in action. None of them had ever seen one before the tragedy.

Intrigued, Tali Nohkati, who had shared his life with animals in the past, approached them carefully. The animals were calm. Their reins hung gently. In spite of the tragedy that he had just survived, he could not help but admire their beauty and grace.

He moved closer. Their tawny coat and their blond mane, still warm from their battle race, welcomed his strokes.

"They must be magical to carry men faster than the wind! They must be sacred to carry them during the battles!" Rakenika said, joining him.

"They brought us sorrow!" Nitis let out. "We should kill them."

"Yes, let's kill them! Let's kill them!" the survivors cried out.

With an authoritative gesture, Rakenika silenced them all and asked Tali Nohkati:

"Do you believe that they will harm us again?"

"I believe we will have to tame them. I believe that we shall absorb their power."

As he spoke, Tali Nohkati grabbed the leather leads. The tribe resumed its journey and the horses, docile, let themselves be led away.

The tribe walked away, under the gaze of Iktomi, the spider.

To avoid being crushed by the hooves of the galloping herd, she had found shelter under a piece of bark, where her nimble legs shaped a new web.

Then, she had tapped on the wood to say: "   ... (May the Spirits of the Earth protect you)." But often, the words and the signals do not reach men. Iktomi, the silent one, knew it too well.

Rakenika was right. The caves, protected from the wind and the icy weather, served as safe shelters.

14 THE REVENGE

As they had left behind their tepees and the mildness of the plains, the members of the tribe came upon the harshness of mountain life. Even so, the majesty of the snow-covered mountain tops and the depth of the gorges fascinated them and commanded both fear and respect in all.

The strangeness of the caves that served as shelter astonished them.

On the walls, their image danced in the light of the fire. Multicolored concretions embellished the vaults.

Strange sounds emanated from the depths. Manifestations of darkness, the sounds of cracking rock and the murmur of underground rivers accompanied their prayers.

Along with their grief, the exploration of the land, the laying of traps and the making of meals filled in their days. Luckily, the game, abundant for the season, healed their bodies.

The loss of Takoda strengthened the friendship between Nitis and Tali Nohkati, to whom Rakenika had given the horses to guard.

Not knowing anything about these animals, they observed them, tried to understand them, talked to them, stroked them. The horses, well taken care of and well-fed, seemingly answered to them and accepted these new masters.

One morning, overcoming their fears, Nitis and Tali Nohkati decided to ride them. Slowly, the animals took them on steep paths, across the woods. At once, the world became vaster, limits were pushed back with every gait, the fatigue lessened.

In the evening, they reported all of this to Rakenika. And Rakenika, who had listened carefully, thought that these horses were precious, even more precious than gold.

On fine days, no one thought about returning to the plains to hunt the bison. Here, the tribe was not short on resources: meat, fish from the rivers and fruit from the forest.

But above all, as they overlooked the valleys, each and every one could see the enemy. As for the dark woods, it formed an impenetrable bulwark.

The attack of the ruthless enemy was still fresh on everyone's mind. The desire for revenge haunted them.

One evening, under a blazing full moon, Rakenika talked:

"The painted men came from the north. Their cruel hands do not knead clay nor grains.

The paths they follow wind along like the reptile and, like him, they hide. But our eyes can see far. Soon, soon we will see them, we will defeat them."

Accordingly, they all started to make arrows, sharpen the knives. The children who were old enough to run whirled the slings.

Rakenika decided they would outwit their enemies by getting rid of the hooves prints of the horses, which only Tali Nohkati and Nitis rode.

Days passed by. But the painted men did not appear. Had they disappeared? Had they conquered other lands?

Taking advantage of the darkness, Coyote inched closer to Tali Nohkati, who was happy to feel his presence. He stroked his fur and gave himself up to the waves of tenderness lavished on him by the animal.

Without a sound, they walked away from the campsite. Evoking the tragedy that had stricken the tribe, Tali Nohkati shared his fears. The hovering threat of an upcoming battle worried him.

But then, Coyote took Tali Nohkati to a rocky spur. The starry night allowed him to see the threatening shadow of the horsemen from the north.

The heart of Tali Nohkati started to race, like a drum in his chest. The boy rushed down the paths leading to the big cave and woke up Rakenika.

The time for revenge had finally come.

Masked by the shadows of the forest or lying low behind rocks, they patiently watched for their enemy, assessing their number, observing their doings.

Under the command of Rakenika, who did not want to lose any of his warriors in the battle, each of them knew what to do. They were ready to leave.

Fall came around. They saw new horsemen joining the campsite. They came back with war treasures, fruit from pillages and violence; food, plenty of food, skins and weapons.

Cheered, beside themselves with happiness from their victories, the painted men sang and danced until exhaustion overtook them.

But soon, the cold night forced them to retreat into their huts and their fires, left unattended, went out. This was the moment Rakenika chose to launch his attack.

In total silence, Tali Nohkati and Nitis freed the horses and gathered them up in a clearing. Next, joining the others, they dug a large furrow around the campsite.

With precise, well-controlled gestures, the women who had followed them poured pine resin and, throwing some embers, lit up the circular vein.

Very fast, an impenetrable blazing curtain rose up to the sky, and all night long, the blaze, poked by a violent wind, took lives, trophies and wooden logs.

Terrifying screams were heard. A few women and children managed to escape. They were hastily caught and made prisoners.

At dawn, only a few smoldering remnants were left of what had been a cruel and bloodthirsty warlike horde.

With his tribe, Rakenika had avenged the honor of the innocent victims of his tribe. He could now return home.

The hope of venturing back to the Land of the Plains made his heart race. But the already impending winter took away his dream.

At the campsite, the captives arrived with worried faces, stared at by those who had brought them down.

Gaho and her fellow women led them into a cave.

After several days had passed, their children, with faces washed of the colors that adorned their eyes, blended in with those of the tribe.

Gaho and her fellow women saw that the prisoners baked the bread like them, that some of their words had the same echo under the walls of the rock.

They also saw that these strangers had nimble fingers, that they knew the art of knotting threads and that their tunics were adorned with mother-of-pearls coming from faraway places.

Thus, several seasons passed. There were no more victors nor vanquished.

The captives became sisters, companions and, through the blood of life, each of them knew that the pangs of childbirth were the same for all women, under the stars and the Sun. But, at the request of Rakenika, one of them, still young and very beautiful, was taken away from the others.

Only Gaho could come near her, feed her and give her proper care and attention.

Tali Nohkati, particularly intrigued by this, wanted to know why. But no one ever answered

Him, and his friend Nitis seemingly did not want to step into this big secret.

When, alone, he was led by his horse, he tried to find traces of Gaho on his path. To no avail. Like a good hunter, his adoptive mother covered her tracks.

As the night caressed the souls, he gently and lightly touched the turquoises and opals, hoping that their light would reveal some of this mystery.

But even the stones, lulled by his heartbeats, dozed off on his warm skin, remaining desperately silent.

15 THE MORNING STAR

The dream of Rakenika became the dream of all. As a good omen, one evening, he announced that this dream was about to come true.

For those who had survived the massacre, the emotions were strong. They would be able to live like before; but nevertheless, the flow of memories and the absence of loved ones would also bring back their sorrow.

For those who had only known exile and for the former captives, there were plenty of questions. But the enthusiasm of the elders was reassuring.

When it was time to leave, winter had not yet receded.

Rakenika decided that is was wiser to anticipate the melting of the snow that made the paths impassable. Furthermore, they had plenty of food. Captured horses had compensated for the lack of game, and the tepees were easy to set up. As for the members of the tribe, in good health, they would have no difficulty overcoming the unforeseen events of the journey.

Led by Tali Nohkati and Nitis, proudly riding their horse, they ventured back.

The scenery gradually changed. The roughness of the rocks disappeared. The valleys opened before them, seemingly unclaimed. The light of the Sun playfully shone through the trees, making the ice-coated branches sparkle.

Suddenly, as they came out of the undergrowth, the vastness of the plains appeared before them.

The children happily dashed towards it, laughing. Some were left speechless. Some started to cry.

Finally, finally, they were back.

From the rumbling ground, the elders knew that spring had arrived. This familiar sound announced the migration of the bison.

Bows, arrows, knives, each and every one sharpened their hunting weapons. Tali Nohkati and Nitis decided to not use their horses to gather the animals together. They were not as skilled as the horsemen from the north, and they wanted to spare their mounts.

When the herd appeared on the horizon, the men, led by Rakenika, regained possession of their old gestures.

The bison were pushed into a narrow channel. Stationed high on the walls that sheltered them from the incessant charging of the animals, the men killed the preys. Once back at the campsite, they all started to work.

To dismember, tan the skins, smoke the meat, make new weapons and hunt the small game. There was plenty of work to do.

But also to pick the berries, the fruit, harvest the three sisters, not to mention playing, running around madly.

As in the olden days, on their generous land, the catches had been numerous. Now the food reserve was full.

There was a big feast. For the happiness, they had recovered, for the last born, they sang, danced and thanked the spirits.

As the night wrapped around them, Rakenika approached Tali Nohkati and confided in him:

"The seasons have whitened my hair, my veins are withering, my strength is slowly leaving me. Soon, I will smoke the pipe with you, and the day after the ceremony of the Morning Star, you will replace me."

Tali Nohkati, moved by the way he spoke, took his hand.

"Father! How could we live without you? You saved us when others wanted us dead. You found me when I was lost. Don't leave us! Don't leave us!"

"I am not leaving you," Rakenika answered, holding Tali Nohkati tight in his arms. "But time is passing by, and it calls for my wisdom, and I know that, from all of us, you are the bravest."

Tali Nohkati gladly conformed to the rituals.

After a fast of several days, Gaho, his adoptive mother, brought him some fruit and fresh water. Her repeated absences had taken her away;

thus he was very happy to see her again. At the dawn of a new day, Tali Nohkati put on a finely crafted buckskin tunic. His opal and turquoise necklace captured the first streaks of dawn. On his belt, he tied the horns of Atsina and on the back of his mount, he placed his bison skin.

Rakenika took him outside the campsite, where all the members of the tribe had gathered.

At the center of a big circle, Tali Nohkati saw a young girl. Probably, he thought at once, the one that Gaho had cared for since the vengeful attack they had carried.

Rakenika stood in front of her, raised his arms towards the sky and proclaimed in a strong voice:

"The Morning Star, a great warrior, leader of men, created the world. The Morning Star and his brother, the Sun, defeated the Moon who wanted to kill all the other stars. For the life that was given to us, for life to constantly renew itself, we chose you, Tali Nohkati, so that you carry out the supreme gesture."

Rakenika entrusted Tali Nohkati with the sacred bow of the tribe and told him:

"You will kill the one who has been the daughter of our enemy. You will pierce her heart with an arrow. Her sacrifice will renew life on our Earth."

Following the orders, Tali Nohkati grabbed the weapon and rode away on his mount in order to deal his blow.

The eyes of all were fastened on him. He bent the cord of the sacred bow, spurred on his horse and dashed towards the young girl.

Entering the circle at a fast pace, he let out a scream that pierced the silence and, faster than lightning, grabbed the one whom he was to kill.

He forcefully held her firm against him.

The horse, responding to the lightest pressure on his flanks, the horse, as if he had recovered his freedom, took Tali Nohkati and the young girl away. And the Sun, triumphant, rose high up in the sky.

At the end of the crossing, as he brushed against the dark line of the horizon, Rakenika and the members of the tribe awaited the return of Nitis.

Astonished, they had asked the latter to go and find the two runaways.

Following the prints left by the horse of Tali Nohkati, Nitis galloped across the plain. Near a river, he found the sacred bow and soon could see the figures of the two runaways, betrayed by a cloud of dust. Under the shelter of a grove, they tried to recover their strength. Leaving his mount behind, Nitis inched closer as would an animal that wants to ambush its prey.

For a long time, he watched Tali Nohkati, the favourite, the chosen one, and the one who was to be sacrificed. In one swift movement, he would kill them both in cold blood.

But, as he grasped his dagger, consumed with the jealousy and hatred that he had repressed for a long time, he thought that exhaustion and hunger would surely be better at it than him. Had Tali Nohkati not shown his bravery in battle? With only one inflicted wound, Nitis would be left with shattered dreams of power and glory.

Therefore, lurking in the shadows, he did not take his eyes off the strangers who called the night to venture into what was still unknown to them: oblivion and death. The day passed by, slow and cruel.

When the Pleiades sparkled in the firmament, Nitis headed back to his own people and said:

"I have ridden across the plain. Near a river, I found the sacred bow. But the water has no memory. It kept no trace of their passage."

Rakenika and Gaho took in those words in silence.

Sorrow fought with insult and gradually turned into profound grief.

Rakenika and Gaho had lost their second son and his absence rendered life unbearable. Which spirit watched over this child whom they had taken in?

Which force had taken the one who made their hearts beat away from them?

If the Earth had taken him as she does with all men, they would have heard his voice in the rustling of the leaves, they would have felt his presence in the warmth of the stones. But the Earth had not taken him and she remained silent.

After days and nights, exhausted, they surrendered.

As a last gesture, Rakenika, in front of the members of the tribe, entrusted Nitis with the sacred bow, the one that, by then, would lead them across the vast plains.

Fall came around, without warning, with its rains, its winds and fogs.

The women bustled around a fire, the tepees set up in a circle. Children ran playfully one after another.

The reserves overran with meat and fruit. The tanned skins were warm and smooth. Nitis stroked his mount affectionately and, contemplating all this, he thought that all was well this way.

16 Until the End of the World

Under the fangs of Coyote, the Morning Star was crushed.

He trampled on the sparkling pieces, scattered on the floor. A source spurted out, next to the one where he had just drunk.

He stood there, on the lookout, watching for any move in the thickets, when the Moon came and landed in between his two ears.

"Here you are, finally!" he exclaimed.

Impatient, he asked her:

"Nuttah and Tali Nohkati are safe?"

"They are! And under a good watch!" she answered. "Raven the crow and Hitchiti the alligator are watching them."

Relieved, Coyote sighed:

"They were so brave. They were so scared also. To be able to run away, they prayed for the night to come and I called you to lead them to a safe shelter."

As his eyes pierced the darkness, many memories jostled his mind:

"However much I swept the dusty floor, I was still afraid that the tribe would find them.

The poor girl was shivering, terrified. Tali Nohkati held her against him, muffling her sobs. No noise was to betray them."

But the emotion overwhelmed him. He could not find the words anymore to express his sorrow and his anger.

The Moon, rolling up and down his spine, soothingly caressed him.

At dawn, climbing up the mountain, they decided to spend some time together. Since Creation, they had barely seen each other.

Thus, this was, down here, a strange season.

The rain started to fall, light and monotonous. In the sky, suddenly forsaken by the Sun, the faint light dimmed.

Everything had seemingly come to a stop.

"If not for this faint light," Coyote said. "I would believe that we came back to the beginning. When we were alone, you and me, when time did not exist."

"In total darkness, we wandered around like lost souls," the Moon said, in turn. "The world did not breathe yet. Thinking that you were getting lost in a black hole, you clung to my hips made of stones. Look! Look at this incredible scar!"

Coyote, intrigued, brushed his paw against the spiral forever inscribed on the Moon by his claws.

"Yes, now, I remember," he exclaimed. "At this very moment, a spark leapt up and, as it ignited a fire, there was light."

"None of us could have said back then what life would be about," the Moon admitted. "We thought we knew it when Tali Nohkati was born, but now..."

The recalling of their protégé suddenly brought them back to reality.

The rain was falling. Imperceptibly, it covered the Earth and Coyote, seeing the water rise, thought:

"All evidence of men will be wiped out. So be it, this way nobody will ever find Nuttah and Tali Nohkati."

When the Flood ceased from above, Coyote walked out of his den. He stretched, shook himself and gazed at the new landscape.

The Moon, the guardian of destinies, confided in him:

"Nuttah and Tali Nohkati rode the waves. On the back of Hitchiti the alligator, through the maze of the swamps, they were rocked by the song of rain showers."

"Therefore, we will be able to resume our journey," Coyote said, reassured. "Under the wings of Raven the crow, turquoise waters interlace. They overflow with flowers. There is a white mountain range."

"On his black wings, dawns dance, stars sparkle," the Moon added.

Happy, Coyote held her back before she traveled:

"Tell me if the hands of our children have played in the streams flowing down to the sea.

Tell me where time will take them."

Joyful, the Moon threw some fiery opals and said:

"They have played. They have laughed, laughing out loud and time will take them until the end of the world, until the end of the world..."

-PART THREE-

It was like at the first days of Creation.
It was the Earth without evil.

17 A New Day

It happened a long time ago.

It happened a long time ago.

Back then, the waters of the Flood erased the footprints of men and covered the Earth. Back then, the Moon deserted heaven, and Coyote stayed by her side.

Still, was it a twist of fate? Was it by chance or out of luck? Nuttah and Tali Nohkati had found shelter in the meanderings of a delta.

The tangle of mangroves formed an impenetrable wall in which Hitchiti the alligator had built them a hiding place.

Like a leaf, the shelter floated at the mercy of the waves, following the reptile's path, under the protective wing of Raven the Crow.

In this makeshift hideout, the teenagers got to know each other. Day after day, curiosity took over fear, worries and sorrow. In the dim light and in their voices, the threads of destiny intertwined.

As for her, the captive daughter of a war tribe, she was to die. But Tali Nohkati had saved her. As for him, after such a long journey and as he was expected to succeed Rakenika, his adoptive father, to become a great chief, he chose to run away instead.

"Why? Why?" she asked.

"Because blood must run through the veins for life to spring," Tali Nohkati answered. As the tribe of Rakenika had wanted to sacrifice Nuttah's heart, these words sounded like a comforting balm, pushing away the cruel images of her utter isolation and loneliness. As she listened to him pronounce these words, Nuttah looked Tali Nohkati in the eyes. She was smiling, relieved. And he discovered the face of this stranger: a graceful face, framed by long, smooth hair, as black as the wings of Raven the Crow.

In their frantic flight, they had left everything behind. Thus, they had absolutely nothing. While the plains were abundant with game, the mangroves seemed very poor to them.

Not knowing anything about this land, they were clumsy. They could not set a fire and, although the continuous stream of rain managed to quench their thirst, it also ruined the sparse food that they could find.

As master of the place, Hitchiti invited them to follow him. Nothing could escape him. Between the roots, he would locate the preys with tender raw flesh. And clac! Between his powerful jaws, fish, shrimp, oysters were caught.

Trustfully, Tali Nohkati and Nuttah went along with him and learned how to fish with their bare hands. Soon enough, the movements of the water and the game of the shadows held no more secrets for them.

The alligator possessed a vast knowledge. As he stood guard, he liked to tell his story. The story before men, when the first drop of water fell.

Lying on the bison's skin that warmed up their sleep, the children listened to him in awe.

Perched on a branch, Raven also listened carefully. The way he talked about the sky in the North enchanted them. The purity of the air, the lightness of the snowflakes, the white mountain tops and clouds, all stirred up some fond memories for them.

The Raven happily flew around and, as he landed next to Nuttah and Tali Nohkati, he told them:

"Here are some eggs. Here are some fruits. Eat! Eat! Tomorrow, it will not rain anymore, and you will leave."

But it had rained for so many days, so many nights that nobody dared believe him. The silence warned them.

All of a sudden, no more flic-flac, no more blip-blop. All of a sudden, the surface of the water, rid of the grains that rippled it, stretched out like a mirror. Happy, Nuttah and Tali Nohkati dove into it with ardor. Under the amused eyes of Hitchiti and Raven, they splashed the waters with their hands. They woke up all the inhabitants of the mangrove, which jumped out, wriggled, chirped and cawed.

Through the leaves, the first sunrays shone a soft light. The golden light of the clear mornings spread again on the world, and that world, awakening from its torpor, seemingly watched out for the return of happiness. Still, no creature could set foot or paw on the ground.

Perched on a treetop, Tali Nohkati and Nuttah all but saw the infinitude of flowing waters. Escaping from the water, streaks of mist rose towards the sky. The evaporation had slowly begun.

But they had to wait. They had to not fall into this cesspool and be washed away by rivers of mud. Intrigued by the course of the streams, Tali Nohkati asked:

"Where are they heading to?"

"To the ocean," Hitchiti answered. "They go and flow into abyssal waters inhabited by strange creatures."

Those words took Tali Nohkati back to the White Land. He thought of Atii the whale. He thought of her belly that welcomed him, of her heartbeats that had marked his extraordinary journey.

"Does the Earth end there?" Nuttah asked in turn.

"The Earth spreads far beyond," Raven said.

This certainty was equally reassuring and worrisome to them. In their refuge made of branches, they confided:

"Which landscapes will we come across? Which men, saved from the Flood, will we encounter?"

But at night, the moans of the forest were their only answer. Finally, in the early morning brightness, the world regained its colors.

Thus, Hitchiti spoke to Nuttah and Tali Nohkati:

"The time has come for you to leave. Raven will guide your footsteps towards the mouth of the delta. If Huracan does not wake up, you will have a safe journey."

The youngsters stroked the scales of the alligator and sadly said goodbye. They thanked him for his valuable help and parted ways.

Under the spread wings of Raven, the refuge that had sheltered them during the Flood still carried them away. A surprising landscape stretched around them. The arms of the swamps widened, allowing manatees to be seen here and there. The flat land bordering the banks welcomed a myriad of birds with richly brocaded feathers. Egrets and pelicans came to nest.

As a soft breeze blew from the open sea, their lips tasted of salt. All of a sudden, magnificent and sparkling in the Sun, the ocean appeared before them.

The Raven landed on Nuttah's shoulders and told her:

"My daughter of the North, my sweet girl whom I have seen being born, I leave you here, with Tali Nohkati. Fate now calls me back to my distant land."

With his wings, he tenderly stroked her hair, her face. As she cried, he added with a sob:

"Don't be sad. Good fortune, for those who know how to seize it, will cross your road."

Tali Nohkati hugged Nuttah to comfort her. As they watched Raven fly away, he led her to the beach. The bright light invited them to join it.

Surrounded by such beauty, their fears dissipated, their hearts beating in unison. Nuttah dashed into the sea, so warm, so delightful. Washing up on the shore, the lascivious waves seemingly waited for them. Tali Nohkati dashed towards them in turn.

They played, having finally found happiness after so many seasons. And when Tali Nohkati looked at Nuttah, when he saw her wreathed in scintillating reflections, he found her pretty.

Coyote knew all that.

Leaving the den where he had stayed, he was also getting ready to resume his journey. One last time, he drank from the spring of the Morning Star. His sharp eyes swept the horizon.

The footprint of the first men had disappeared. But the Earth, his Earth, created fruit and flowers again.

The perfumes already teased his nostrils, carrying him towards the valleys and plains. The Moon had resumed her course in the sky. Tali Nohkati and Nuttah laughed out loud. Walking along the banks of a river, with soft clay stuck in his paws, Coyote was happy, very happy. And he thought that all was well.

18 THE ISLAND OF CAGUAMA

Life took its revenge with lavish displays. On this bank, summertime seemed endless. The sea abounded with fish. The trees offered their tasty fruit while providing refreshingly shaded spots.

Nuttah and Tali Nohkati had weaved some fish traps to catch fish as well as thin walls to shelter their dreams. At the end of the day, they kindled a fire. The glow of the flames, conducive to confidence, made the opals and turquoises of Tali Nohkati's necklace dance. But, although Tali Nohkati enjoyed talking about his past adventures, Nuttah could sense that he would not share the secret of the stones.

She talked about her former life. When the tribe launched attacks; when, under the command of her father, the men came back with exceptional loots. Back then, she was just a child, but her memories were intact, her words precise.

Sometimes, words became sparser, and they would look up at the stars. Tali Nohkati, recalling Rakenika's teachings, told Nuttah about their journey through the sky, and the magnificent sky sprinkled its grace.

They fanned the fire and the glow of the flames, providing guidance to the lost ones and sending signals, like calls into the night.

But, at sunrise, Nuttah and Tali Nohkati could see nothing but the horizon, infinite and absolute; nothing but a seemingly endless white shore spreading out; nothing but a fine sand beach, immaculate and silent, in the clear air of dawn.

At the end of a fishing day, the skin of the bison had welcomed their tired bodies. Tali Nohkati had fallen asleep, but Nuttah had trouble sleeping, kept awake by the wind whispering through the leaves and the rolling waves.

She stood up. Under the brightness of the full Moon, she saw prints on the floor. She inched closer. The prints were big. Revealing a regular movement, they seemed to come from the sea and went up the beach.

Surprised, Nuttah followed them for a while when she heard a short breath. She was about to call Tali Nohkati when she heard:

"Come closer! Come closer!"

The sound of this voice coming from nowhere startled her. Her heart was racing. She was going to run and alert Tali Nohkati, but, worried to not see her by his side, he had already joined her. He too had heard the voice. In spite of the reigning darkness under the trees, they carefully moved forward.

Moving aside to let in a ray of light, they could only distinguish a massive shield crawling at ground level with extreme slowness. Then, a deeply wrinkled head emerged, scaring them. Remembering the words of Hitchiti, Tali Nohkati wondered if that was Huracan waking up. The animal, as to answer to him, let out:

"I am Caguama, the turtle!"

Nuttah and Tali Nohkati attentively observed her. They did not dare move, not knowing what to do.

The beast was very strange. Where did it come from? What was it going to do? Was it lost? Those questions gnawed at them and the beach, so welcoming yesterday, suddenly frightened them.

Nuttah and Tali Nohkati were not alone anymore. But as they thought they would meet men, this odd creature stood in front of them instead.

The turtle seemed exhausted. Compassionate, they approached her. Tears ran down the furrows of her withered skin. She whispered:

"The life that I carry in me is ripping me apart. With my feet, I must dig a nest. Alas! I am losing my strength. Would you lend me a hand?"

At once, all fears evaporated. Nuttah and Tali Nohkati helped her dig a deep well and soon, before their astonished eyes, Caguama laid her eggs, one by one.

In the half-light, her precious seeds appeared, white and shining. Between her groans and sighs, time seemed suspended.

Yet, at the crack of dawn, the stroking Sun spread its first rays.

Caguama gently covered up her fragile treasure with warm sand. Then, in a final attempt, she turned towards the sea. Exhausted, she decided not to resume her journey back to the ocean depths. She stayed next to those who had helped her.

Tali Nohkati and Nuttah let her rest. They were about to go fishing when Caguama confided:

"None of your fellows has ever lived on these lands. Here, the winds and currents are the only masters. Here, the capricious delta sweeps away everything in its path."

This revelation stopped them cold. Perceiving their fears, Caguama added:

"Don't be fooled by the sweetness of the life you have found down here, after the Flood. Between heaven and earth, there is an island where some men live, an island to which I can guide you."

Downcast, silent, Nuttah and Tali Nohkati understood that they would have to leave again. Only, sailing out onto the ocean requires skills and wisdom. As she regained her strengths, Caguama would continuously encourage them. Day after day, she provided guidance: how to choose a tree to build a boat, how to decipher the movements of the swell and the shape of the clouds, how to find their way under the Milky Way.

One morning, everything was ready. Loaded with provisions, the small boat waited. Slowly and steadily, the turtle began to mark her wake. Tali Nohkati finished loading his bow and arrows, the horns and bison's skin. Nuttah tied up her jet black hair. As she adjusted her headband on her forehead, she saw a pearl. Resting on a pile of dry leaves, its reflections danced playfully in the brightness of the day. Nuttah picked it up and rolled it in the palm of her hand. It was smooth and looked like the snowflakes of her childhood. She stored it in the warmth of her chest and joined Tali Nohkati.

The moment had come to leave.

Led by Caguama and pushed by the trade wind, the small boat moved slowly away from the shore. Carried by the gentle wind, Nuttah and Tali Nohkati left forever their former life and childhood. Worried, she huddled up against him. Drawing on his travelling experience within the bowels of Atii the whale, he comforted her. And as he took her into his arms, he caught a glimpse of the pearl within her tunic.

Tali Nohkati thought of the Moon. She had probably appeared while Nuttah slept. She had probably stroked her face, so soft, so beautiful. Tali Nohkati felt the eagerness of his soul lifting his chest, and he thought to himself:

"I loved Rakenika and Gaho who took me in. I loved Nitis and Takoda like brothers. But when I look at her, my heart softens."

19 His Name is Taino

Pushed by the trade winds, the small boat moved away from the shore.

On the ocean, flooded with light, Nuttah and Tali Nohkati steadily headed South.

Caguama, the turtle, swam in front of them. The swell and currents held no secret from her.

At twilight, the first night looked equally strange and enchanting.

In the vastness of the world, suddenly invaded by darkness, the Moon poured down her soft light.

Just like a golden and silver compass, she provided guidance to Nuttah and Tali Nohkati through the maze of the starry sky. All this beauty filled their hearts with hope.

"Isn't it wonderful! Isn't it wonderful!" Nuttah said, smiling at Tali Nohkati.

"It's magnificent!" he answered, holding her hand.

Moved, they sat still one next to the other. Rocked by the gentle touch of water against the hull, they tirelessly gazed up at the sky. Then, Tali Nohkati felt his heart begin to race. Words of love gathered behind his lips, eager to be pronounced. Unable to stand it any longer, he embraced Nuttah and kissed her.

She received this enchanting kiss with delight, seizing it with strong emotion as life wanted it this way. In the splendor of the night, her hair, like the sea, captured the brightness of the nova. Her skin had stored the warmth of the Sun. Her hand caressed the face of Tali Nohkati.

She stroked the face of her beloved one, who was so brave. Affectionately, she called him "Kitchi, Kitchi". And the words of Raven the crow came back to her. Fate, luck had brought her to him. These manifestations of destiny led her now to happiness. Maybe Caguama the turtle knew all of this. In the morning, she had not reappeared. In the morning, she had swum into the darkness since the man and woman who had saved her, now had become one.

Nuttah and Tali Nohkati sailed, constantly taking turns to maneuver the small boat and rest.

The clear sky and mild winds made their journey effortless in parts. Sometimes, fish fluttered around them, seemingly guiding them.

But for several days, nothing broke the blue line of the horizon.

Nuttah was sound asleep when land finally appeared faraway.

Tali Nohkati woke her up at once.

Deeply moved, their eyes stayed fixed on this spot, feeling equally fearful and hopeful. All of a sudden, the currents, like invisible hands, carried them westward. Dolphins leapt out of the water and shapes began to take form with the appearance, here and there, of a rocky spur, of a weaved fringe of foam. They moved closer.

Birds wheeled around and dove into the sea at warp speed. They moved even closer. The coast became visible, magnificent under the Sun, revealing a stretch of light sand. Waves washed ashore while a dense vegetation bordered it. They moved closer.

The swell, stronger at the entrance of a channel, carried them further ahead. They could already see slowly swaying trees when, suddenly, a figure of a man walking along the shore appeared.

This man, Nuttah and Tali Nohkati had imagined, saw them. He stopped walking. He carefully watched the small boat sailing up to him. He seemed to hesitate for a short moment, but his curiosity took over. He walked forward into the water until it reached his waist.

Trustful, Nuttah and Tali Nohkati, still carried by the swell, waved at him. The small boat ran aground, and the man helped them set foot on the beach.

Dressed only in a loincloth, the one who welcomed them was tall and strong. His skin was marked with tattoos. A cord hung from his neck, holding a few shells.

He talked to the strangers, secured their small boat, and helped them unload the few goods that they owned onto the sand.

Nuttah and Tali Nohkati, happy to have reached land, thanked him and expressed their joy to be there.

Amidst the heat of the moment, their eyes met. Their words jostled together, mingling with their confident gestures. Then, the man pronounced a few words that were left without answer. He repeated those words, thinking that Nuttah and Tali Nohkati had not heard him. But, suddenly, speaking different languages created distance between them and they fell silent. They looked at each other, not knowing what to say anymore.

Surprised, the man searched their face and wondered: "Who are they? Where do they come from?"

He looked at their goods. The bow was the only familiar item. The others, he had never seen before: a big dark skin, horns, a stone necklace with watery and fiery colors. He had never seen such things.

Tali Nohkati tried to reassure him. He invited the man to touch all of the objects. He named everything. The man, intrigued, tried to understand these strange expressions. Then, Nuttah laid her hand on Tali Nohkati's chest and exclaimed:

"Tali Nohkati! Tali Nohkati!"

Then, she laid her hand on her chest:

"Nuttah! Nuttah!"

The man nodded. He gave a hint of a smile and, laying his hand on his chest, he said:

"Taino! Taino!"

At its zenith, the Sun shone in all its brilliance. Taino guided the woman named Nuttah and the man named Tali Nohkati away from the shore towards some salutary tree shade. Then, he cooked a meal. On a bed of embers, he cooked some of his catch: beautiful, multi-colored scaled, leaf-wrapped fish. He had given them coconut water to drink and limes to bite on. It was delicious!

Curious, Taino pointed out to the sea and the frail, small boat. Tali Nohkati guessed his questions. With the help of a thin branch, he drew a horizon line on the sand. On each side, he drew clouds and raindrops falling on a hut. Revolving around this scenery, several suns and moons.

A few steps away, he drew a turtle. Then, he drew the small boat on the sea. Taino looked at this drawing and seemed to understand. He repeated every word that Tali Nohkati pronounced, trying to memorize them. Tali Nohkati did the same when Taino pronounced them in his language.

Time passed. Shadows gradually covered the lines that had been drawn on the beach. Strange sounds were heard coming from the inland, but the dark body of leaves prevented them from seeing where they came from. Since they would not venture out further, Nuttah set up a campsite for the night.

A sudden darkness engulfed them. The star-studded sky and the fire were their only guides.

Tali Nohkati and Nuttah found out that, in this part of the world, the Moon was upside down, and the night seemingly half-smiled.

Taino pointed out the stars and told them that, the next day, he would take them to his tribe. But tomorrow was far away. The ground, warmed by the day, welcomed the worn-out bodies. The song of the wind and the murmur of the waves rocked them to sleep.

Taino stood up abruptly and searched his baskets. He threw a thick rope around a tree trunk, then around another one. He patted the suspended white fabric that swayed in the breeze. He came back to Nuttah and invited her to lay down on it.

As he met her incredulous gaze and that of Tali, he laid down on it, mimicking his satisfaction with exaggeration. Laughing out loud, he kept saying:

"Hammock, hammock! Hammock, hammock!"

20 The Men from the Delta

When Taino returned to the tribe along with Nuttah and Tali Nohkati, all the members hurried to see them. Bombarded with questions, he gave a detailed account of their first encounter. Alerted by the commotion, a man appeared at the door of a big hut. Taino approached him respectfully and resumed his story.

Dressed in a loincloth with hair adorned with flowers, the man listened attentively. He persistently stared at the strangers, in an attempt to determine the reasons which had led them there. In spite of the trust that Taino seemingly expressed towards them, the appearance of these strangers and the objects they carried intrigued him.

Tali Nohkati approached him in turn. He laid everything that he owned at his feet, inviting him to discover his possessions. And, as he did on the beach, he drew on the ground the adventures leading to his arrival to the island.

He punctuated his illustrated journey with words that he remembered from his conversation with Taino. Those words, clumsily pronounced, caused some laughter, but the man appreciated them. Eager to learn more, he invited Tali Nohkati to carry on.

Besides the crossing and the Flood, Tali Nohkati realized the man wanted to know where they originally came from. Thus, he drew various landscapes and animals: mountains, plains, bison and other animals. Eager to show the limit of this vast land, he traced two lines as a symbol of a large river. The large river subsequently divided into a myriad of rivers, which intermingled to eventually flow into the sea.

The mention of the delta particularly unsettled the man and those who watched him.

Silence fell abruptly, and along with Taino, they all wondered: what is Caney, their chief dressed in a white loincloth, his hair adorned with flowers, going to do? What does he think of these strangers? Is he going to accept them? Reject them?

As they all held their breath, Caney approached Tali Nohkati. He laid his hand on his shoulder and told the crowd:

"Give them enough to eat, drink and dress. This man and this woman will stay with us."

As he heard those words, Taino joyfully took Tali Nohkati and Nuttah across the village so that everyone could meet them. And not far from the plot of land where he lived, he invited them to settle in.

Nuttah and Tali Nohkati, happy to be taken in, laughed with him. Together, they built a palm leaves roofed hut.

Mabi', Taino's companion, rushed to give them a hammock. Nuttah joined her to cook the meal and the first night fell.

Nuttah sank into sleep, but Tali Nohkati stayed awake. In the hut that sheltered them, he put away the objects of his past life. Next to the entrance, he hung his bow and the horns. Then, he rolled up the heavy bison skin, thinking it would come handy in the winter. But days went by and the winter never came.

In this sunny land, the sea was generous. The forest offered its game, fruit, and refreshing waterfalls. Some pieces of land were farmed. Rain would often fall at the end of the day, providing the land with its daily water intake. Nothing was missing.

Women took care of children and picked up shells. They also picked up the manioc and wove baskets and hammocks. The skills of Nuttah and her knack for jewelry conquered Mabi' and her new girlfriends.

Men hunted and fished, at times leaving for days. Tali Nohkati's experience proved valuable. His agility and patience along with his nice catches convinced the members of the clan. Caney always asked him to come along with Taino and the men whom he chose for the big hunts.

Time peacefully slipped away. From now on, Nuttah and Tali Nohkati could speak the language of those who had taken them in.

Around the fire that gathered them at sunset, children played, and they each took turn recounting their days. With their faces illuminated by the flames, they relished the tales of Nuttah and Tali Nohkati's travels before the big rain.

Caney enjoyed listening to them. Beyond the sea, all seemed so strange. Their words reminded him of the voyage that he had set out on with his people. But Caney did not let his emotions show. He kept quiet.

One evening, as Tali Nohkati laid next to Nuttah, he felt a presence. Was it the full Moon that played with the shadows? Was it the rustling of the branches that disturbed his sleep? He rose up to check.

His steps took him to the beach. The milky-white light of his distant friend undulated on the waves as the languid sea unrolled its mother-of-pearl drapes onto the sand. Tali Nohkati's eyes never grew weary of that sight. The beauty soothed him when a hand laid on his shoulder, startling him. Caney, who was not far from him, had joined him.

"Are you waiting for someone? Are you expecting something?" he asked, intrigued.

"No," Tali Nohkati answered.

"Are you trying to see your old shores?" Caney asked insistently.

"The waters from the sky and the earth have destroyed them forever."

"Who knows?" Caney whispered, adding: "When your words fill the night, I think of our lives back then."

His revealing comment surprised Tali Nohkati. Therefore, the men who had taken them in were not from here. Then, where did they come from? On which land had they left their footprints? Guessing his thoughts, Caney invited Tali Nohkati to follow him. A path took them to the steep foothills of the island.

In spite of the thick vegetation, Caney's eyes could make the path out in the dark. They soon reached a wind-battered plateau summit. Several cavities could be guessed on the rocky wall against which he leaned on. Holding a torch, Caney entered one of them.

What Tali Nohkati discovered left him speechless. In a riot of colors, some fantastical faces made funny faces. Ceremonially dressed warriors entered in the order of battle. Temples rose up into the skies. Birds flew around the Sun. In an interlacing of prodigious trees, feathered reptiles fought big cats with black markings.

With every flicker of the flame, the extraordinary images took Tali

Nohkati back to Zia Zia the snake, and also into a new world. A world that Caney had known very well. Driven by his memories, he recounted the adventure that led him and his people from the extraordinary cities to the depths of the forest.

"Like Nuttah and you," he said, "We walked for a long time, to finally sail for days and days through the mangrove and on the sea. Like Nuttah and you, we are the men from the delta." Suddenly, in the brightness of the sacred cave, an army of dead bodies appeared. Mummified, attired for their ultimate journey, they sat tightly against each other, their legs tucked under, their arms crossed over their chest. Forever silent, they seemingly contemplated their past life. Tali Nohkati discovered then that he was not at the end of the earth as he had believed.

With Caney, he turned towards the fresco representing the river and the meanders of the delta. He grabbed a charcoal, traced the same lines, and as to teach, marked their island between them.

Moved, Caney and Tali Nohkati looked at the drawing that resembled two hands holding each other. Two hands of men carried away by destiny.

21 AT THE CROSSROADS OF WORLDS

During this time, Coyote stood at the crossroads of worlds.

On the strip of land connecting the northern lands to the southern lands, the Moon wanted him to meet her. They had not seen each other since the end of the Flood.

"Kitchi! Nuttah nicknamed him Kitchi! Nuttah, so beautiful!" Coyote whispered.

"The echo of their happiness makes the stars jiggle," the Moon said.

Coyote contemplated the moving, quiet sea.

"The air is sweet, pure. But men? Are men good? Are they gentle with them?" Coyote asked.

"Yes. They gave them coconut milk to drink. They gave them manioc and guava to eat."

Coyote let those reassuring words comfort him. He wondered how tasteful these foods could be when he suddenly rose up on his paws.

"I am not a good swimmer. Unless I let myself be carried away on a drifting tree trunk, I will not see them again," he lamented with regret.

"Assuming the trunk drifts away in the right direction!" the Moon pointed out. "Wouldn't you rather lift yourself up onto my shoulders?"

"If my old carcass would ever fall, the ocean would gulp me down faster than I gulp down my favorite field mice!" Coyote exclaimed. "But I cannot get used to the idea of not seeing them anymore."

Giving him no time to think, the Mood, already, pulled him up on her side. And being reunited again, in the middle of the night, brought them back to the time of their youth, when there was nothing, when the world had no voice.

No sooner had he arrived on the island that Coyote, impatient, dashed through the foliage. He finally found Nuttah and Tali Nohkati.

In a suspended woven cotton hammock, they slept in each other's arms.

Seeing them this way made Coyote leap for joy. From a higher branch, he leaned over them, breathed in the sweetness of their flesh, gazed lovingly at the beauty of their souls. He held back his barking to not disturb their sleep.

Curious, aroused by the smells and sounds of this new land, he prowled around. He smelled the fruit and sweet potato baskets. He listened to the rustling of the treetops, the whispers of the breeze, the murmur of the river.

Pleased with it all, he bounced back again to them. Then, noticing the coming of dawn light, Coyote left a precious stone by Nuttah's side and quickly rejoined the Moon on a rocky outcrop. He lifted himself up back onto her shoulders and said:

"I will come back with you! I will come back with you! The waves we have created will not swallow me!"

The Moon, joyful, soared into the skies. She laughed, spreading her metallic brightness. She rolled here and there, faster than light, towards the crossroads of worlds.

22 COKI

After hearing the revealing comment from Caney, Tali Nohkati, bewildered, had rejoined Nuttah and fallen back asleep next to her. When he awoke, with Nuttah still asleep, he found an emerald. The presence that he had felt was then real. He tried to find traces of Coyote's visit, but to no avail. How could he have come to this island? Tali Nohkati thought. The nearest land is waves and waves away from here, and my dear friend is not a good swimmer.

Seemingly guessing his thoughts, Nuttah, opened her eyes, took his hand and said:

"In my dream, I saw him running. The Moon wanted to show him something and was ahead of him. The warm air of the night carried their laughs."

At those words, Tali Nohkati pointed at what he had found next to her. Nuttah, surprised, laid the emerald next to the pearl. The mother-of-pearl, playing with the morning lights, captured the deep green of the stone.

Delighted, Nuttah rolled them in a dark wooden bowl and, putting her finger on her lips, she whispered:

"Guardians of our secrets, I will put them together and keep them on my chest."

"Which secrets are they supposed to keep?" Tali Nohkati asked.

Nuttah curled up against her beloved and said:

"As the day rises, a life grows inside me. As the Sun owns the world, a life owns me. Nine moons will pass, and our child will see the light."

Tali Nohkati, ecstatic, tightly held Nuttah in his arms and kissed her. Days went by.

Tali Nohkati saw the belly of Nuttah grow rounder. As he placed his hands on it, he could feel the child move and see the copper-colored skin of Nuttah ripple with the rhythm of his movements. He remembered the time that he had spent within the body of Atii the whale. From her inside, only her heartbeat and the song of her voice connected it to the world. The women of the tribe, attentive, watched over Nuttah. Taking turns, they took her to bathe in a cool running spring and massaged her body. As Nuttah usually joined them to pick up shells or proceed with the weeding of their plots of land, the women asked her not to.

Therefore, she made a hammock in which to put her child and embellished a large loincloth to carry the baby on her back. Then, she let herself be lulled by all the happiness that surrounded her and that enhanced her beauty.

When night fell, she experienced strange conversations. In the torchlight, her dimly lit belly closely resembled the faraway planets. The Moon then landed in front of her and Tali Nohkati, surprised, heard them whisper.

What did they tell each other? Where did the words come from that he could not understand? What was the mystery?

She made him think of his mother. At times, she came back in his dreams, that no one else could see but him. Had she also talked with the sky?

Days went by, shining under the Sun, shimmering in the evening showers. The tree frogs were singing in the heart of the forest when Nuttah squeezed Tali Nohkati's hand. A sharp pain made her wince.

The time had come! He called Mabi' and "those who know". He called the spirit of joy for Nuttah to give birth without pain.

When the child was finally born, Tali Nohkati laughed and cried at the same time. Holding her in his arms, he approached the shore and bathed her small body in the lukewarm seawater. The tree frogs kept singing in the forest. Happy and proud, Kitchi looked at his daughter at the dawn of her life and called her Coki.

Under the Sun, in the rain, fate spun its web. Coki grew on the island of Caguama, next to the women and men of the delta. Nuttah and Tali Nohkati adored her. Coki was their happiness, the fruit of their love.

They had adorned her neck and ears with iridescent mother-of-pearl.

In the privacy of their home, the child learned life simple gestures and, soon, she joined them. Nuttah taught her how to crop manioc and fruit, how to spin cotton. Tali Nohkati taught her how to prey on fish and small game. They taught her how to respect what the generous mother nature had given them.

With the other children, she had fun, ran and played. Their laughter skipped about everywhere, gushing down the waterfalls, rolling in the waves, jumping from branch to branch. Coki, agile and light, had conquered the spirits of water and of the forest.

Under the Moon, under the stars, fate spun its web.

Coki liked it, in the evenings, when they all ate together by the fire. The flames rose up against darkness, casting lively shadows against the sand.

Mesmerized, she listened to the story of her origins. The White Land of Raven the crow and of Yupik the bear, the vast plains of Iktomi the spider and of Atsina the bison, the glowing red desert of Zia Zia the snake and the mysterious mangrove swamp of Hitchiti the alligator, filled her dreams.

Her gaze filled with wonder, she watched her mother dance as she used to long ago to celebrate the victories of her tribe. She watched her father mimic his hunts of the past.

Her world was magical. Her world was big, bigger than her, bigger than the ocean, bigger than the sky.

Coki, cheerful and mischievous, had conquered the spirits of the wind and of the night. Sometimes, she would go alone and explore every corner of the island.

As light as a bird, she wandered here and there. Sometimes by the waterfalls, sometimes on the plateau that bordered the cliffs. She could effortlessly climb up the steep foothills leading to the outcrops. Hence, the island held no secret for her.

Caney had caught her a few times, worried about her running away from her tribe. But he always found her back in the evening, by the fire, happily curled up in the arms of Nuttah or of Tali Nohkati.

As he headed to the sacred cave one day, Caney saw her, her arms full of fruit. He followed her, intrigued. When she entered the cave, he thought of stopping her but what he saw unsettled him so much that he decided to step back.

Coki had lit a torch. In spite of her young age, she fearlessly approached the dead, offering fruit to each one. Suddenly, she stopped in front of one of them. Her small hands caressed her hair and the skeletal face. Next, she started talking to her. Her clear voice filled the cave with a long forgotten sweetness.

Was it magic? Was is a message from the hereafter? Under half-light, the mummy, seemingly coming back to life, became animated and answered the child. Moved, Caney could not take his eyes away from the strange dialogue.

When he saw her walking down to the shore, tears were running down her cheeks. "Why these remains?" he wondered. "Did Coki know that, before, this soulless body was that of Coya, the great Queen?"

In the sanctuary, silence was the only answer to his questions. Coki was already back. Nuttah tenderly fixed her cloth, Tali Nohkati kissed her cheeks. In the sunset, they went for a walk by the sea. Coki laughed, stopped to listen to her bouncing heart. And her heart said: I am beating, here and now. Tomorrow does not yet exist.

23 HURACAN

As a sign of a new cycle, thousands of birds coming from beyond the sea wheeled around the island mountain tops. Thousands of them landed on the cliffs, nesting there, offering abundant food.

As the undisputed head of the tribe, Caney gathered his best hunters.

The paths leading Tali Nohkati, Taino and the others bordered vertiginous drops to the valleys below. The climb, full of pitfalls, was slow and perilous. Upon reaching the lands that touched the sky, they organized their camp. Next started the beating game. Setting up an ambush, the men started to select their preys. Gifted from their ancestors, the miraculous manna was sacred. Caney decided on a number for each so that when the moment came to share, nobody would be forgotten.

Soon would be the time for the great dance. The dried and smoked meat would strengthen the bodies. The feathers would adorn the hair. Songs and prayers, through them, would rise up to Heavens.

At the end of this first hard day, the men gathered to dine. Some soon fell asleep. Tali Nohkati's thoughts took him back to Nuttah and Coki, when he caught Caney staring at the horizon. The full Moon emitted its soft light and his gaze lost itself to infinity.

"What was he waiting for? What is he watching out for?" he wondered, intrigued.

Often he had caught him in this position, standing tall, like a rocky spur, facing the ocean. At times, a tree trunk or a drifting body would wash up on the beach. Caney would rush to them, stare at the face, bang at the wood in search of its origin. But what he believed to be messages carried by the waves would remain motionless for eternity, forever lifeless and silent.

Dawn found the hunters pinned to the ground. A strong wind, along with torrential rains, started to blow during the night.

In the leaden sky, streaked with blinding lightning, violent gusts of wind gradually swept up everything in their path.

The men, prisoners of the mountain tops, had tied themselves to one another in an attempt to form a shield against the repeated assaults. But the incessant battering of these raging blows painfully challenged them.

Falling down violently, the hailstones scratched their faces, hammered their bodies. Powerless, the men witnessed the death of the birds, carried away by the storm. But, thinking of the children and women they had left behind, their hearts hurt even more.

In the din of the storm, Tali Nohkati could hear the plaintive voice of his companions repetitively saying: "Huracan! Huracan!"

This word, continually coming out of their mouths, wreaked havoc amongst them.

"Huracan! Huracan!". Suddenly, when all he could think of were Nuttah and Coki, he remembered. Hitchiti the alligator. Hitchiti, the guardian of the mangrove and of the delta, had told them: "If Huracan does not wake up, you will have a good journey."

But who was that monster that came pouring down on them? Where did he come from? Why would he fall on them this way? No later than yesterday, the sun was shining. No later than yesterday, they were all together. They had a good life under the Sun and the evening showers. So why? Why?

His suffering opened old wounds that he thought had closed forever: the fiery wind that took his parents, the tragic end of Atsina the bison, the separations, the loneliness, the attack of the people from the North, the revenge, the sacrifice of the Morning Star, the escape into the mangrove.

Then, the faces of his two loves brought him back to the heart of the hurricane. Where were they? Could they take shelter? These thoughts haunted him.

He was alone with all his companions, completely alone in the midst of this vast ocean where nothing could seemingly restrain the wrath coming from beyond the world. Anguish and pain lowered the resistance of Tali Nohkati. But he fought back as much as he could. He fought to not fall into madness and to feel alive, in spite of the horror.

After several days of battling a one-sided fight, the defeated men finally perceived a glimmer of hope. All of a sudden, the cleared sky became vast again and the wind stopped at once.

On the plateau, carcasses of birds lay strewn, and a profound silence reigned. Rousing themselves, the men hastily untied the ropes that had kept them together. They picked up the few tools that had not been swept away and headed back.

On the path ravaged by mudslides, they went back in an unbearably slow manner as their walk was hindered with each step. They finally reached their camp.

Before their eyes, there was nothing but desolation. From the tangle of fallen rock and uprooted tree trunks, they could distinguish, here and there, some pieces of cloth or gourds.

These touchingly lonely fragments of broken objects did not reassure them. In spite of their utter exhaustion, the heart of the men was racing. Their bruised hands brandished sharp weapons to cut through the entangled branches, as they all called for their family. Alas, from this hellish chaos came no sign or sound of human presence.

Soon, nightfall overtook their search. In spite of their courage, the men did not have the strength to continue searching anymore. Nothing of their former life remained. On the shore, Caney lit a big fire, shared the fruit they had found. He took turns talking to them, found comforting words, and finally sat by Tali Nohkati's side.

Along with their companions, they sobbed silently. Then, Caney, overcome by grief and sorrow, held the hand of Tali Nohkati and told him:

"My friend, my brother, a piece of me died for the second time. A piece of me died for the second time."

Was it a dream? In the night, a trembling hand lay on Caney's shoulder. He grabbed it and took the frail body that approached him next to the glowing red embers.

Mabi' was looking at him, her lips in a slight smile. Happy to see her alive, Caney hastily woke up Taino, who hugged her. Very soon, the men circled around them. Caney rekindled the fire and Mabi' told them:

"You were already far, on the way to the mountain tops when the wind started to blow. The women were looking for shells, and the children were playing on the beach. I was picking up healing herbs in the forest with Coki. Above our heads, the trees bent as if crushed under the hand of a giant. I wanted to find shelter, and I called Coki to head back. Alas! Alas! The rumbling of the ocean and the howling of the wind covered my voice and, in the dark forest, I could not see her anymore. I looked for her, I looked for her. But a violent gust of wind blew me away and, hit by a branch, I lost consciousness."

Her voice charged with grief floated above the flames. Tali Nohkati and the other men listened to her, strongly moved.

"When I opened my eyes, the world around me was devastated and silent. It took me several days to return to the shore and Coki, Coki whom I was still looking for, whom I was continuously calling, did not answer me."

Mabi' had to stop talking. Exhausted, she could not find her words anymore. As they listened to her, the men understood that they would not see their wives and children again. Yet, Tali Nohkati was still hopeful. If the forest had saved Mabi', maybe it had also saved Coki. Not being able to wait anymore, he decided to resume his search. A few companions joined him and, under Caney's lead, they set off once more.

Under the streaks of dawn light, they could see, in the chaos of trees and branches, some small footprints. They led them up to the entrance of the sacred cave.

Afraid to offend the ancestors, the men had come to a halt. But Caney and Tali Nohkati regained their strength. They ran towards their only hope of a future.

24 The Words of the Ancestors

Rays of sunlight softly lit the walls of the cavern and the face of Coki. Tali Nohkati leaned over her. Her peaceful breathing reassured him.

She was sleeping on the bison's skin, next to the opals and turquoise necklace. Atsina's horns seemingly wanted to defend her and, in the familiar wooden bowl, he saw the pearl and the precious stone.

Coki woke up and clung tightly to her father's neck. She recognized Caney and smiled at him. Her face, full of life, made their heart race.

Bewildered, Tali Nohkati wanted to know. How did she end up here? Who had brought those objects to which he was attached? Coki did not answer his questions. Pointing at the lined up deceased, she simply said:

"I hid with them. I fell asleep with them."

Caney was also puzzled. But he did not dare interrupt the unhoped-for reunion. Without delay, the three of them headed back. Once in the campsite, everyone gave Coki whatever food they had left. She was hungry and did not seem surprised to only see Mabi' and the men. Suddenly, she turned towards the sea:

"Mommy is there. They are all there."

Mabi' and the men listened to her attentively, eager to hear more. Then, looking towards the other side of the island, she held the hands of her father and of Caney and added:

"As for us, this is where we will go."

These words unsettled the survivors. Tali Nohkati remembered the moment of his initiation when he was cast away from the community. He had fasted. After several days, exhaustion and hunger had caused strange visions. Coki, luckily isolated from the rest of the group, must have lived a similar experience.

She had probably perceived some sounds or seen some images. She had probably dreamt. As for Caney, he took it as a message. He was sure of it, Coya, their great Queen, had chosen Coki. Beyond death, she had elected her to accomplish a destiny. But he remained silent, choosing to rather take care of his family. The presences of Mabi' and Coki had given the men some courage. In no time, they had restored what could be and, in the communal house where they, by now, all lived together, they supported and encouraged each other.

In the surroundings, although the plots of land could not be cultivated anymore, the sea still offered a few catches. Still, it had all become too clear. Living here was not possible anymore.

One evening, as they had hunted for some game in vain, Caney said to the survivors:

"Tomorrow, we will cut down the tallest trees. We will build pirogues, we will dry some fish, we will make calabash gourds and store water."

"Where will we go?" one of the men asked.

Caney turned toward Coki. She was standing by her father. With a soft voice, she answered: – "Where the bluebirds fly around the Sun. Where stone steps rise towards the sky. Where palaces keep the secret of the stars."

Quivering with emotion, they all looked at her, puzzled. How did she know? Which power was looking down on her? What ancestor had expressed himself through her?

None of them dared to ask. None of them wanted to break the spell. But since the child had talked, they would leave.

Caney had chosen Tali Nohkati to oversee the building of the vessels. He came from the sea, and his knowledge was invaluable. Day after day, Tali Nohkati lavished advice. Skills that he thought he had forgotten came back to him. Little by little, under the admiring gaze of the men, Mabi', and Coki, the vessels took shape.

The elders prepared the provisions and wove the sails.

When the rain, so welcome yesterday, fell on their work, they patiently waited, watching the sea.

Tali Nohkati seemingly drowned in it by staring at it so much. Caney, who used to do the same before, approached him and confided:

"She never gave me back those whom I loved. Do you remember all those long nights when I was awake? I waited for my beloved wife and son. In vain! In the waves, on the shores, I did not find them. Today, all I have of them is a vague recollection that I keep in the deepest part of my heart."

This unexpected confidence moved Tali Nohkati.

"I am lucky," he whispered. "I have Nuttah who smiles and sings in my soul. I have Coki, who looks like her so much, by my side."

Caney nodded and added:

"Along with Mabi', our memory keeper, Coki is, from now on, our only hope. Her miraculous presence calls for respect and her youth orders us to leave again."

"She is just a child!" Tali Nohkati said. "All I want for her is a nice life, marked by tenderness."

But I know too well how fate often, too often, treats us roughly."

"This may be to counter it that the living owes an eternal rest to their ancestors," Caney said.

"Before leaving, will you help me seal the entrance of the sacred cave?" Caney asked him. Tali Nohkati agreed.

The moment of departure approached. They all sat between the fresh water and the food. The boat slowly rocked to and fro. With a wealth of experience behind him, Tali Nohkati would lead them. Mabi' and Coki would sit by his side. Caney would be in another pirogue. For the journey without return, they would follow one another, stay together, tie one another up if needed. That is how they had decided to do it.

Caney and Tali Nohkati checked on the last details. Then, with a sharp blow, they broke the moorings. Everyone held their breath. The vessels quietly sailed away on the clear water. Little by little, the vast ocean surrounded them and their island, so beautiful on a horizon splashed with blue glitter, vanished forever.

At the same time, at the crossroads of worlds, the Moon landed on Coyote's backbone.

They did not need words to understand each other. They simply knew. They would stay together too. They would stay for these survivors.

Following the course of the Sun across the sky, Tali Nohkati steered South. Favorable winds filled the sails. Soon, the first stars would appear. Their twinkle would fill the men with wonder. Mabi' would name them and tell a story for each of them.

Coki sat on the bison's skin, next to the opals and turquoise necklace. Atsina's horns, as well as Tali Nohkati's bow and arrows seemingly wanted to defend her. In the wooden bowl, Nuttah's pearl and emerald gently rolled with the movement of the waves.

In the blue glitter of the ocean, Tali Nohkati proudly watched his daughter. He was very happy to love her so much. He could hear his child's heart bouncing. He thought of all the happiness that life had given them all the same, of all the happiness that life would still give them.

Next, he thought of the deceased who had watched over her, of the Moon rays, and of the footprints of Coyote that he had discovered in the sacred cave.

– PART FOUR –

« So said Tochihuitzin
So said Coyolchiuhqui
We come out of the dream suddenly
We only come to dream
It isn't true, it isn't true
That we come to live on the earth,
Like grass in spring
Is our being.
Our heart makes them grow,
Flowers sprout from our flesh.
Some open their corollas,
Then they become dry.
So said Tochihuitzin
So said Coyolchiuhqui. »

25 THE ISLANDS THAT DANCE

If Huracan had not forced them to do so, the men would have never left their land.

But Huracan, a cruel and violent wind, had decided otherwise. Huracan had swept everything in its path, taking away and forever those they loved. Listening to Coki's words, the child chosen by the ancestors, the survivors left the island.

Led by Caney, their undisputed leader, and by Tali Nohkati, the stranger whom they had adopted, they now sailed southwards. As they sailed the vast ocean, they tried to overcome their grief, clinging to hope for a new life.

Without respite, they scanned the horizon in search of a hospitable shore. Caney and Tali Nohkati took turns at the helm. The movements of the swell, the course of the stars, and the changing colors of the waters all indicated the path to follow.

Tali Nohkati was about to rest briefly when, suddenly, his beloved daughter Coki pointed out in the distance a narrow dark green strip of land lying between sea and sky.

Alerted by the child's joy, Caney and the others stared at what seemed to them a hint of a still uncertain future.

Finally, they reached the end of their long journey. Finally, they had arrived somewhere.

Caney ordered to stay on course, and, slowly, the vessels sailed ahead, pushed by the warm breezes. The line on the horizon seemed to spread into infinity. The currents of a powerful tide began to carry them into the flow of a vast river.

At that moment, Caney, summoning his memories, recognized the shapes of a familiar landscape from the past. Moved, he announced that they had returned to the branches of the delta that they had left a long time ago. And he pointed out, here and there, the islands that dance. Scattered by the mercy of the waves and covered by an evergreen vegetation, the sandbars escorted the men.

Some elders recalled names and images in swatches. But for those who had only known their island splashed by light in the heart of the world, the rustling sounds and the colorful landscape they encountered provoked both fear and curiosity.

This river was so vast. Where was it? Where did it end? Which men lived here? Did they look like them?

To avoid being caught by the night, Caney ordered the vessels be drawn in. The bay that he chose was wide and shaded by tall trees. Hastily, the men found a safe spot and, immediately, some left in search of food while others built a shelter.

They could hear unfamiliar sounds from all around. Soon, darkness fell over their new territory.

In front of their fire, Caney said:

"Tomorrow, we will go and explore the meanders of this river."

Some faces expressed fear. But fatigue overcame the survivors and sleep won them over.

As Tali Nohkati sat by Coki and dear old Mabi', the only surviving women, Caney approached him and confided:

"The jungle that surrounds us is like the sea, infinite, impenetrable and often cruel. Yet, some men live there. We must find them."

As he spoke, he looked at Tali Nohkati and the souvenirs from his former life: the skin and the horns of Atsina the bison, his opals and turquoise necklace, his bow and arrows. Then, he saw, in the wooden bowl, the emerald and pearl of Nuttah, the gone forever wife of Tali Nohkati. Under the dim light of the Moon, the gems gleamed magnificently.

At dawn, Caney and a few men set off. The islands that dance would not allow for a permanent stay, therefore they had to find the other men as soon as possible. When they reached the sound, they drew alongside dry land. Step after step, they walked deeper into the forest. Under the vegetation, the Sun had vanished, and its scarce drops of light were barely enough to show them the way. With machetes, they cut their way through the deep forest. They advanced slowly and with difficulty, but they bravely continued.

Tali Nohkati had never seen anything like it. Gigantic trees soared to the sky, seemingly scratching it. Massive lianas coiled themselves around the branches. Loud roars and strange rustling sounds put them on alert. Yet, Caney kept going, leading his companions with songs. And some, recognizing ancient laments, sang along with him.

At times, Caney came to a halt and called. In full alert, he waited. Then, he called again. Tali Nohkati watched him with admiration. Where did his friend draw his strength? And also, what was this language that he had never heard? Who was Caney calling? What did these refrains mean? Were they prayers to the Gods? Were they the names of those he looked for?

He was absorbed in those thoughts when, suddenly, a man appeared. Young, dressed in a simple loincloth, a bow on his shoulder, he stood at the top of a protruding root. Silently, he observed the hikers, nothing escaping his hunter's eyes. This encounter was expected and hoped for. Yet, once surprise was gone, worry took over. Was this man following them? For how long? Was he alone?

Caney approached him. From the quiver containing his arrows, he pulled out a headband made of colorful feathers and put it around his forehead. When the man saw the headband, his face lit up. He stared at Caney and pronounced a few words.

Caney answered, and under the astonished gaze of his companions, the man kneeled before him to show his respect.

The hunter exchanged some words with Caney, then he guided the men across the forest.

Soon, a clearing appeared before them. Huts formed a big circle, with women and children standing in the center. As soon as the latter saw one of them with strangers, they called and were at once joined by men. Bombarded with questions, Taquari, the young hunter, told what had happened. As they heard the story and saw the set of feathers that Caney wore, the members of the tribe were astounded.

Intrigued, their leader Bororo approached. With a penetrating gaze, he sized up Caney and those who came along with him. Where did the men who spoke their language and looked so much like them come from? Curious, he invited Caney to speak.

Surrounded by his companions, Caney told their story. Their land, in the middle of the sea, shimmering in the Sun. The abundance of fruit and the peaceful days in spite of the sorrow of exile. The joy of the great hunt.

The night fell slowly. Burning torches lit up the camp. Caney was still talking. The terror of Huracan, the vanishing of their spouses, the grief that tore apart the soul of those who stayed. The embalmed bodies of the deceased Queen Coya and of the ancestors, attired for the great journey. Finally, the words of Coki, the child prodigy, and the crossing into the islands that dance.

Putting words into action, Caney drew on the ground the pictures that adorned the sacred cave. Fascinated, Bororo listened to him, looked at him. Every word, every image made his heart skip a beat. An emotion that he thought long forgotten overwhelmed him.

In front of him stood a brother. In front of him stood, brave and proud, a man from the old promise. But how could it be?

At the end of the story, Bororo took out a case that he had forever treasured and did what he had not expected to do. In a solemn gesture, he adorned his forehead with the same feathered headband as Caney's. At the heart of the deep forest rose a loud sound. As before, the people of Coya were only one. As Fate decreed.

26 THE PEOPLE OF COYA

From that moment on, they lived together.

Those, who until recently were just survivors, had found their place amongst the other members of the tribe. The men formed groups of experienced hunters. Ties of friendship were forged between Bororo, Caney and Tali Nohkati.

Tali Nohkati, the stranger who came from beyond the seas, inspired curiosity. The features of his face, his journey across the great plains, and his escape with Nuttah fascinated those of the great forest. His daughter Coki became the subject of much attention. Along with Mabi', she received tenderness and comfort from the women. They became inseparable, learning to grow plants and gather new fruit.

Sheltered by the tall trees, their days passed by peacefully. Blue macaws and laughing monkeys had adopted them. However, the forest was dangerous. The people of Coya knew it well. While it fed and protected them, the inextricable jungle could also kill whoever violated its laws. They all feared the sharp fangs of the jaguar, the constrictive strength of the anaconda, and the ferocity of the piranhas.

To separate men and wild animals, a ring of fire encircled the huts every evening. From dusk to dawn, nobody was to walk through it. Yet, one night, in the deafening silence of the forest, the Moon, Coyote and Yaguara the jaguar crossed it.

While men were sleeping, Yaguara said:

"I have followed the people of Coya and I have seen. Walking down the mountain, every one of these men, every one of these women planting corn. They all ate its dough, blond like the Sun. They gathered mango, lime, passion fruit."

Coyote, laying down on his side, listened to him. The Moon nestled in between his ears.

Yaguara added:

"On the fertile plateau, children grew, became strong. They built temples, prayed for the rain to fall. Tupis, running away from other lands, poor men and women who were exiled, took shelter on their land. I saw the guardian of their harvest. The people shared the water, the corncakes and the fruit."

The words took form on the golden disc of the Moon. Yaguara added:

"Together, they chose their king. Then, one day, Coya was born. Alas, came also the time to fight. Greedy people from other lands devastated the fertile plateau, rooting up trees and corn plants."

Coyotes, standing on his four paws, listened to him. Yaguara kept talking:

"I have seen desolation and hate. Blood left the bodies of men, spilling into furrows, taking in its path souls and seeds. In spite of the king's death, those who had built the kingdom bravely brandished their broadswords. In this chaos, Coya grew up. Her beauty mesmerized those who knew to look at her. Along with her brothers and sisters, she fought the battle."

The words marked the reddening disc of the Moon. Yaguara finally said:

"Then, the enemy leader captured her. He wanted her to belong to him, forever submissive. But, helped by a shadow that masked her, she could stab the tyrant's heart with a frayed blade. Thus, with this act of bravery was born Coya, the queen. Alas, misfortune kept on striking. A cold ocean current reinforced tides and winds. The dried land became barren, and the people were forced to leave."

Coyote listened and the story, word after word, became forever incrusted on the black veil of the Moon. In the morning, the fire had gone out.

As soon as daylight broke, Tali Nohkati, who felt Coyote's warm breath in his neck, had erased all traces of Coyote and put away, within the folds of his bison skin, the three engraved plates of the Moon he had found next to him.

In the dim light of dawn, he prepared his bow to hunt and some fruit to take with him. Caney and Bororo joined him. With them, he was going to finally cross the great forest and find the original paintings that decorated the cave of his ancestors.

They entrusted Taquari, the young hunter, and the other men with the task of watching over the tribe and set off at once.

With each step, branches entwined them, trees swallowed them. Bororo knew every inch of this impenetrable jungle. Rustling, calling and buzzing sounds held no secret.

In this hostile environment, walking was laborious. Sometimes, there was no day or night. The only thing that marked time was hunger. In hammocks, they rested. But they could not linger too much. They had to keep walking, keep walking relentlessly.

Rain regularly pounded their bodies and their footprints. And always, the damp cloak of mist wrapped around them, hiding the sky.

At times, they would find the river that had brought them from the sea. However, they would walk away from it, under the command of Bororo and slip through the jungle darkness.

This journey reinforced their friendship. In the tangle of branches, they were only one. The animals of the forest watched them. Some of them even followed. Yaguara the jaguar and Jiboia the anaconda. The big cat and the reptile, both powerful and dangerous, seemingly watched over them.

Bororo, the undisputed leader and guide knew it; just as he knew that, soon, their old kingdom would appear.

Suddenly, Bororo stopped and took his companions to the top of a tree. And there, before the astonished gaze of Tali Nohkati, a pyramid rose from the heart of a vast plain.

Moved, Caney told him:

"This is where our life was. This is what men and time took away from us."

Resurfacing memories flowed back into the minds of Bororo and Caney. Their gaze embraced the whole world that they had just found again. They laughed, hugged each other and cried, all at the same time. Eagerly, they started to pace their old city up and down while Tali

Nohkati, fascinated, discovered this new world. They looked for traces of their past in this deserted landscape. The plain, once full of people and their culture, was now overgrown by tall grass. Here and there, Bororo could make out the shape of a neighborhood; Caney, the banks of a canal. On the esplanade of the pyramid, where ball games used to take place, a disconcerting silence prevailed. Solitude had taken over the territory.

Tali Nohkati followed them, touched the cut stone walls and tried to picture the river that had flowed through, carrying the objects described by his companions: fruit, fabrics, gold and precious stones.

Carved stelae stood in all four directions.

"They were the guardians of our journeys," Bororo and Caney confided.

Suddenly, in the heart of Tali Nohkati, all the paths that he had crossed intersected: from the blue-tinted ice of the Great North to the forests inhabited by wolves; from the vast plains to the scorching deserts and the waves of all the oceans.

"Is that what men's destiny is about?" he wondered. "Leave, always, leave, whatever happens, to other lands, to find other men?"

"Tomorrow, we will head back to the forest and tell them that the enemy is no longer here." Bororo announced.

"We will say that the deserted city is waiting for our return," Caney added.

At the end of the day, they finally laid down to rest. The shadow of the ruins was by no means threatening to them. Instead, like a familiar beast, it stretched out next to them as it followed the course of the Sun. Already, the stars gathered to fill up their night of dreams. Lying low on top of the temple, Yaguara and Jiboia were on the lookout so that nobody could disturb their sleep. Ferocious sentry, they watched over them under the sky as guardians of the last parchment of the cycles and destinies.

27 THE DREAM OF THE FEATHERED SERPENT

The three men brought back bits of pottery and a piece of red fabric inlaid with gold and jade, that they had found in the ruins. Gathered around them, the members of the tribe tirelessly listened to the story of their discovery, while they looked at the relics.

The design represented on the fabric left no doubt. Bororo, Caney and Tali Nohkati had found the ancient city. Every member inched closer to see and touch the vestiges unaffected by the passing of time. It was not much, but what appeared before their eyes was reminiscent of the paintings that Caney's men had drawn in the sacred cave on the island.

Coki, who regularly visited with offerings of fruit and flowers, pointed it out. The image of Coya the queen and the other deceased, attired for the last journey, came back to her.

Fixed in eternity, these ancestors stared at the drawings on the petrified walls that once were their story, one that she did not know then. Yet, with the shifting shadow and light of the day, the emaciated features of these mummies became animated, seemingly coming to life.

Before a puzzled Coki, fantastic warriors engaged in battles on the painted stone walls. In a riot of colors, strange and marvelous animals ran, bounced. Some even gracefully danced and spun around.

Bororo sat next to her:

"As I remember, this piece of fabric belonged to the coat of our Queen."

Coki laid her hand on it and stroked it. Under her touch, the gold and jade gleamed, emitting a gentle warmth. She looked up at the leader and said:

"As I remember, the same fabric dressed the sides of Coya in the sacred cave. At dawn, the rays of the Sun set it aglow and brought it back to life."

They all listened to her. Coki added:

"Dawn is an auspicious time, it inspires hope. One morning, I saw. The fruit and flowers I had left behind had not withered. In the arms of Coya, they were still beautiful like the first day. I thought I had heard: "Beyond death, as I hold these offerings, I will keep my promise." But, who had said that? Wasn't it rather the echo of the sea or the breath of wind?"

Tali Nohkati, disconcerted, looked at his beloved daughter. She had grown so much!

All the hardships that she had had to suffer did not alter her grace. Nuttah, her forever gone mother, had passed her courage and beauty on to her.

At once, Bororo and Caney entrusted her with the precious fabric and gave the departure signal. It was finally time to go back!

They parted into different groups to walk through the great forest. Tali Nohkati and Taquari, the young hunter, would lead one. It was not an easy task. They had to guide, feed and protect. But the joy of going back to the ancient city and, for those born in exile, to discover it was so great that it made them forget about the dangers that loomed.

In baskets and sacks, the women carried their children and goods. The men, bows in hand, led and closed the group. At its zenith, the light of the Sun fell on the leaves in shafts, easing their progress. Animals ventured into the campsite from now on abandoned. Their footprints gradually erased those of the members of the tribe and, already, the embers from their previous fires mixed with the earth.

In the darkness, Yaguara and Jiboia followed the men. Proud and silent, they escorted the feathered snake, the magnificent and legendary lord.

At the end of a long day walking, Coki settled for the night with her companions. While they were asleep, she could see through the tangled branches, a twinkling wreath with changing colors. Puzzled, she inched closer.

This mysterious bouquet sparkled under the canopy of the forest. A myriad of multicolored fireflies fluttered from here to there. The air was filled with a delicate scent that wrapped Coki in freshness. Charmed, she inched even closer.

Under the branches, Yaguara and Jiboia, whose presence she did not suspect, watched her every move. All of a sudden, the feathered snake appeared. He snatched Coki and took her away. Trapped, her heart leapt in her chest. She tried to scream, but the vision of this fantastic animal left her speechless.

"Don't be scared!" he said to her hastily.

"It is you that I saw in the cave!" she exclaimed, as she recognized the animal. "So, you really do exist!"

Lighter than air, he flew around her. His feathers brushed against Coki's face and adornments.

"I am what men hope for. That is all I am. What is real is the sharp fangs of Yaguara and the fatal constriction of Jiboia. What is real are the days that come back and take you there, beyond the mountain tops and plains."

"Still, I can see you," Coki said. "You are here, in front of me. I can hear your soft and melodious voice. You dance in your adorned, silky skin."

"You can see what the Stars weave. All you can see are shadows carried by light. The Sun and the Moon, in their mad course, enjoy surprising you."

Astounded, Coki asked:

"But, if you are not, how could you possibly bring me here?"

The feathered snake looked deeply into Coki's eyes, put a finger on her lips and whispered:

"I am only a dream!"

As suddenly as they had appeared, the sparkling bouquet, the jaguar, the anaconda and the feathered snake had vanished.

Now, only the night haunted this part of the world. The silver Moon rays, from high up in the sky, pushed the branches apart, casting light here and there, on the menacing darkness. Coyote, perched on her shoulders, sniffed her footmarks and reassured her.

But it was Taquari, the young hunter, who found her in the morning. She was laying on a bed of soft moss.

"How did she get here?" he wondered.

Since she was deeply asleep, he did not wake her up. He merely looked at her, aware of her regular breath. Delicately, Taquari lifted her up in his arms and back to his other companions, who were still sleeping.

With a soft cloth, he wiped the multicolored beads from her forehead, hence erasing all traces of her nocturnal escape. As he did, he found strange feathers in her hair. He had never seen such feathers! Yet he knew all the birds of the forest. He carefully collected the feathers one by one and put them away in a case that he slipped into Coki's belongings. He heard a faint flapping in the air.

Coki opened her eyes. The Sun had now risen. The group was about to leave to the city of the stones. Taquari, who watched over them, led the way. His companions followed him joyfully, walking at a good pace. Already, they could see a clearing. Taquari laughed with them and Coki. Coki, such a beautiful keeper of mysteries.

28 THE CITY OF STONES

Coki kept her dream to herself. Coki did not reveal anything.

Taquari, who walked along with her, also remained silent. In the clearing that welcomed them, the group came to a halt. But just for a little while as they eagerly resumed their journey. Some even picked up the pace.

Soon, the first stones came to sight. And, all of a sudden, the ancient city appeared.

Under the Sun at its zenith, the imposing ruins were impressive. The men and women paced it up and down, walking along what was once the surrounding walls of palaces and temples.

They met up with those who arrived before them, and now, they were here, all together.

Already, the children dashed into the new territory, eager to explore. The men and women bustled about. From the forest, they brought plenty of game and fruit. The evening meal was going to be joyful.

At nightfall, Caney and Bororo invited the whole community to gather around a big fire.

The delicious meat gave them strength. The fresh water tasted like hope. The limes and mangoes were sweet like the evening breeze.

The sky, spangled with all its stars, shared their joy. Some stood up and danced, like before, when they were happy. Caney and Bororo joined them.

Tomorrow, they would rebuild the city of stones, dig canals, irrigate the fields. They would adorn the sacred stelas with gold and gems. Tomorrow would be happy and, along with his companions, Tali Nohkati was hopeful. Together, they eagerly set to work to rebuild the city. Put the houses up, weed, redefine the alleys, fill in the silos, bring the water back, replace the potteries, find and restore the paintings. There was plenty to do.

Every day was filled with a new discovery or suddenly brought back a memory. Little by little, the city came back to life.

Tali Nohkati was dazzled. Man of the woods and plains, having lived only in rustic huts, he marveled at these constructions.

Nothing could be seen through the lodged blocs of stones. They were seemingly assembled by giants.

Once the canals were working again, Caney asked him to accompany him. Following their heart, they entered the forest again. Soon, they left their frail boat. There, the astonishment of Tali Nohkati grew greater.

In gigantic gaps, bottomless wells overflew with crystalline water, of an incredible limpidity. Where did it come from?

"This precious water is that of the Creation," Caney said. "The generous rains irrigate our fields, but this one comes from the bowels of the Earth."

Tali Nohkati recalled the basin of white rocks that he had seen in the desert. In the solitude of rocks scorched by the Sun, Zia-Zia, his friend the rattlesnake, had shared with him the secret of the Birth of the World.

Here, in the casket of the emerald jungle, breathtaking landscapes could be seen through the transparency of the water. The underwater walls gleamed with iridescence. Thin seaweeds, rocked by a current that came from the depth of ages, slowly undulated.

Tali Nohkati was enthralled.

But, as he followed Caney back to the city of stones, he saw, on the ground, familiar footprints studded with turquoises.

He carefully put them away in the case containing his arrows and thought about the uninterrupted thread of a fragile life.

Time passed by. The echo of the builders had spread beyond the faraway lands, and Tali Nohkati saw new faces.

Men and women coming from the high plateau, hardened by the wind and the cold, were welcomed as they used to be. Their arms came in handy. Carve or dig up, excavate or sculpt, there was plenty to do.

Through them, Tali Nohkati discovered new worlds. He did not grow tired of listening to them.

"There is," they said, "an impassable mountain where only eagles live. There are signs on the ground, drawn by an army of giants. There is a mysterious temple, long ago abandoned, that brushes the sky. And even further, there is a big ocean, so vast that no one will ever dare crossing it."

From then on, Tali Nohkati lived in a house made of stones, with thick shield like walls. The warm fire offered a soothing glow. The oil lamps spread a dim light. The shared meals included corn breads, tomatoes, potatoes. They often had eggs and meat. The fruit was simply picked up from the trees in their garden.

He, along with his fellows, had never lived this way. Digging into his memories, he could not recall such an art of living.

Before his eyes, his beloved daughter grew bigger every day. She teased him, laughing now at his first white hair. She freely enjoyed her father's tenderness. And the latter discreetly watched over her.

They all had appointed her as the spokesperson of the ancestors. Hence, she held an important position within the city.

Under the leadership of Caney and Bororo, groups had formed. There were the groups of the learned, the warriors and the others. Everyone had their place. Tali Nohkati had his place with the ones who know. His past experiences made him a wise man, but he was insecure.

At times, when alone with his daughter, he would ask her:

"Did the ancestors reveal something to you?"

Coki would look at him and answer in a low voice:

"The dead do not speak. According to their dreams and hopes, the living are the ones who believe that they can hear them. Yet, I do not know how, I do not know why, when our lives wander off, they enter our bodies and let us know."

Time passed by.

Throughout the seasons, the tribe of Bororo, the survivors of Caney and the inhabitants of the high plateau had blended their blood. The mix resulted now in a great and strong people. The years were marked by the crops and the celebrations, the hunting and the prayers. Mabi' had left, slowly, to meet up with Nuttah and all the others in this other country, unknown and uncertain. Taquari, the young hunter, had become a man and his love for Coki made him handsome and proud. When he came to ask for her hand, Tali Nohkati accepted with good grace since the one who had found them in the forest had never failed.

The city of stones, thanks to the faith of those who had founded it, thanks to the courage of those who had rebuilt it, gleamed under the skies. She was the center of the world and the world was hers.

The palaces and temples rose above the treetops. Precious and spellbinding, their golden and azure paintings told the stories of mankind by torchlight. Beneath the stars, the stelas, erected in the four directions, seemingly carried the sky.

At times, in the silence of the night, Tali Nohkati visited them. North, south, east, west, all the paths that he had traveled crossed here. Remembering Coyote, and gazing at the Moon, he thought:

"This is where my journey ends. It is here."

29 THE CORONATION OF COKI

The needed rainfall came back. Born in the clouds, they made the rivers rise. And the rivers, overflowing with silt, gushed down the high plateau slopes, their floods enriching the land. From everywhere men's prayers raised up to the skies, asking for bountiful crops.

But that year, rainfalls of a rare violence swept away blocks of stones, trees, destroying plots of land everywhere.

Alarmed, Caney and Bororo went to see Tali Nohkati. As unsettled as they were, he was not a bit surprised when he heard them say:

"Coki must go to the temple. She must call the attention of our ancestors and ask for help."

He left at once. He walked through the narrow streets of the city. The ditches were overflown, the trees were dripping, the canals were on the verge of overflowing. The downpour brought him back to past times, when he was sheltered in the mangrove swamp with Nuttah. The incessant rainfalls had then protected them. But it also reminded him of the deadly Huracan.

If, unfortunately, the gusts of wind and the showers kept on blowing and falling onto the city as they had on the island of Caguama, their newly found joy would be lost forever.

On their doorsteps, the inhabitants helplessly witnessed the devastation brought by the storm. As they recognized Tali Nohkati, they encouraged him and expressed the same request as Caney and Bororo.

Tali Nohkati reassured them as much as he could. When he finally knocked on his daughter's door, she was already ready.

Escorted by Taquari and her father, Coki entered the sacred walls alone. The crowd that had followed them found some makeshift shelter and somehow camped out, at the bottom of the high stone walls.

Despite the rainfalls, Coki reached the summit of the temple and scanned the curves of the valley. Bolts of lightning tore the sky apart, thunderclaps stroke the world.

The jaguar and the anaconda, keepers of the book of destinies, laid in wait, in the dark. What did she do for days? The sanctuary, in the hands of the mighty weather, was devoid of any offering.

What could she see in the midst of darkness?

In this sanctuary, exposed to all winds, there was no ancestor resting. Attired with her gems, still, she prayed. She prayed for the storm to pass, for the Sun to come back and for the corncobs to grow. She fasted in the cold and in the silence of the walls.

Here, no paintings to delight the eyes, no torch to guide the steps. Here, nothing and nobody to fight with her.

What could Coki do against the raging wind blows, against the ravaging assaults of the storm? Nobody knew, and nobody dared to ask. The whole community, gathered around Caney and Bororo, waited and hoped. Tali Nohkati, toughened by years of struggling to live and survive, supported Taquari, worried that he would not see the one whom he loved anymore.

Holding it all in, he also feared not seeing her anymore. More than anyone else, he knew how fragile life could be and fear gripped him. The rain fell, again and again. All was devastation. Coki could not see the fields, the roads nor the trees of the great forest anymore.

Finally, in the middle of the night, overhanging the storm clouds, she saw the tip of the Moon crescent. A last drop of rain glided down her arm, and she started to feel a soft wind on her face.

It was over. Already, there, the bright dawn repainted the sky. There, the golden Sun swept the horizon.

It was over. She took off her precious outfit and went down, one by one, the steps leading to the heart of the city.

There was, like a miracle, a glimpse of light. The still silent earth, overflowing with water, exhaled mist patches.

Wreathed in pale and floating veils, Coki appeared before the astonished gaze of the crowd. Taquari and Tali Nohkati rushed towards her to hug her. Then a huge clamor arose. Like a miracle, the light came back and everyone, relived and freed from the wrath of the skies, expressed their joy.

On the way to the damaged city, each of them rushed to see her, to show her gratitude. Surrounded by her family, she answered with a sweet smile, waving. The wave of fondness made her heart race, and she thought of her long-gone mother.

If only she had been here, she thought, if only she could have hugged her and shared this moment of happiness with her. Alas, fate had decided otherwise. Since it was the master. Prayers or offerings could not do anything. She certainly knew it now.

At her doorstep, Caney and Bororo welcomed her and showered her with praise. Then, with authority, they directed the people to clear out the city, repair, come back to the fields.

Day after day, the city regained the luster of its former days, and soon this episode was nothing but a bad memory. But Caney remained vigilant. Just like Tali Nohkati, he knew that, here below, nothing ever lasts, nothing ever stays the same. Just like the friend whom he had welcomed, in the past, he knew that fate does not care about much and often falls upon them. Still, he wanted to give thanks. He called the elder council. In order to obtain the mercy of the weather and to answer the expectations of the people of the land, they had a stone tablet engraved:

"At the full harvest moon, Coki, the one who talks to the ancestors, Coki, the one who reads in the clouds, Coki will become our queen. At the full harvest moon, we, the people of Coya, will bless her and honor her till the end of her reign."

At the full harvest moon, Coki, the one who talks to the ancestors, Coki, the one who reads in the clouds, Coki was sacred Queen. At the full harvest moon, the people of Coya kneeled down in front of her and honored her.

Her beauty was unmatched. Her beauty, a reflection of her origins, gleamed by torchlight. Dressed in a red and golden linen wrapping cloth, she walked with dignity. Feathers of extraordinary colors that none had ever seen before adorned her gracefully, pulling up her black hair. Jade rings encircled her ears, neck and arms. On her forehead, a white pearl looked like the daughter of the Moon.

Tali Nohkati proudly wore the testimonies of his long journeys: the skin and horns of Atsina the bison, his necklace inlaid with opals and turquoise, his bow and arrows.

Caney and Bororo wore their colorful feathered headbands. And the people of the high plateau adorned themselves with multicolored fabrics.

Coki walked in front of them, towards the temple, holding, in the palm of her hand, the sacred emerald.

Alone, she climbed up the stairs leading to the top. There, she laid down the precious stone, a symbol of life and love.

In the sanctuary, offered to the mercy of the weather, exposed to all winds, in the sanctuary devoid of paintings and torches, Yaguara the jaguar and Jiboia the anaconda, keepers of the book of destinies, watched over her.

30 THE IMPOSSIBLE DREAM

Felicity. Felicity. The word constantly came back to Caney's mind.

Often, he walked away from noise and from the crowd. Then, he watched, not the city that he had abandoned in the past, but the one that he had rebuilt with his companions.

He said to Tali Nohkati, who had joined him:

"Despite the grief and the memory of beloved ones forever gone, I am proud and happy. The lofts abound in provisions, there are no enemies at the borders. This recovered prosperity brings me peace."

He added:

"Today, my heart could not beat anymore for anything else. I have hoped too much. I have waited too long to see this dream swept away by a hostile hand or by the wrath of the Gods."

As the day ended, the first stars appeared. Caney looked towards the temple where thousands of torches glowed.

"Your daughter, our Queen, carries within her the secrets of this happiness," he suddenly confided in Tali Nohkati. "Her reign has to last for a long time so that nothing comes to disrupt this peace. Her reign must be pure so that her prayers can rise and reach the skies."

Then, he whispered:

"Fate is too often cruel. And, in the evening of my life, I do not have the strength anymore to face it once again."

The evocation of Coki had unsettled Tali Nohkati. On his way back home, he recalled her coronation.

As he escorted her to the temple, he had not prayed. He had not invoked the skies.

"My daughter, my happiness and that of Taquari have nothing to do with the restored felicity," he thought to himself. "She carries within her the same hopes as ours, and her reign will last only as long as her life."

In the half-light of his edifice, he lit the stone walls. He laid down on his bison skin but had trouble sleeping, his thoughts drifting along with his torments.

All of a sudden, he saw a familiar shadow. Coyote. Coyote was here. Tali Nohkati, happy to see him again, kissed him, stroked him, becoming once more the child he used to be.

He said to his loyal companion:

"You know it, that life gives practically nothing. It shows its different faces. By turns cold and white, warm and red, soft and green, tender and blue, mysterious and dark. Sometimes, only sometimes, it gives us the most beautiful of all. But most of the time, it shows us the cruelest of all."

He added:

"What can prayers and offerings do when the elements of nature are unleashed? What can our complaints and revolts do when death is taking us? We, the men, are too weak to fight against them."

The voice of Tali Nohkati was soft.

"I have known Rakenika, my adoptive father, great leader to all. I have known Takoda, my chosen brother, great hunter to all. Despite their strength and courage, they laid down their arms. Despite love and wisdom, they gave in. Under the yoke of the enemy or of grief, there are no winners in the fight against the passage of time."

Finally, Tali Nohkati fell silent. He had fallen asleep. Coyote, standing on his paws, came to lick his face and cuddle up to him.

The Moon came next. As light as a flower petal, she landed on his forehead to travel through his dreams and lighten his heart.

Tali Nohkati was still sleeping when a clamor rose from everywhere. Carried by the first winter fog, it raced down the hillslopes, across the harvested fields and orchards. At the crack of dawn, it ran, from alley to alley, reaching the banks of the canals. All along the banks, voices clamored it. On their doorsteps, each and all stepped out to catch bits and pieces of the clamor.

Soon, on the great temple esplanade, the crowd gathered. Caney and the elder council looked at the men and women walking hastily towards them, seemingly wondering: is it true?

Caney waived to answer their question and announced:

"People of Coya, today, peace and happiness are ours forever." From the crowd rose a cheer of joy. "Coki, our queen, the holder of our ancestors' secrets, will stay in the temple to pray. Coki, eternal sovereign, will stay there forever to honor the Gods and, through her offerings, thank them for their kindness."

As he heard those words, Taquari, drowning in the crowd, felt dizzy and started to stumble.

He attempted to extricate himself from the crowd, but already the multitude rushed to the steps of the temple, dragging him along, to take on the sacred sanctuary.

Coki was going to be locked up. Coki was going to be walled up alive. Taquari, in a blind rage and overwhelmed with anguish, felt his heart racing. He was carried away by these men whom nothing and nobody could stop. Seized with madness, they jostled, shouted. Some fought to be the first ones at the top. When Taquari finally managed to free himself, he ran through the deserted and silent alleys. He ran to Tali Nohkati, who was still sleeping. His toneless voice tore Tali Nohkati out of his dream. His words cut through his heart, and reopened old wounds.

At once, the world around them collapsed.

Holding onto each other, they tried to contain the flood of their devastating rage and grief. They would save Coki. But how? The jubilant crowd surrounded the temple. Its euphoria, kindled by the fiery preaching of Caney, made it dangerous. In spite of their desire to free their daughter, spouse, what could the two of them possibly do, faced with the people of Coya? Nothing.

Wisdom required them to wait. Wait for the exhilaration to die down. Wait for the streets and squares to empty from all its inhabitants. Nighttime may be of some help. Summoning up their courage, they aimed at somehow offering one another support. Tali Nohkati gathered their belongings. A few things, in truth, but all that had represented their life. In wicker baskets, they put food and water, the skin and horns of Atsina the bison, the bow and arrows, the set of turquoise, the emerald and pearl of Nuttah. Taquari added the strange feathers that adorned

Coki's hair in the heart of the woods. They would have to hurry, hide, leave without a trace. And not expose themselves to the slightest chance of being caught.

On paths they did not know, the two men knew that after freeing Coki, fate would take them forever elsewhere.

31 UNDER THE WING OF THE CONDOR

Night finally fell.

Tali Nohkati and Taquari rushed towards the silent city. Their shadows glided without a sound through the deserted alleys, and soon, they found themselves at the foot of the temple.

They were about to climb its first steps up when, suddenly, Yaguara the jaguar appeared before them:

"I was waiting for you," he let out. "Let me take you to her."

Surprised, Tali Nohkati and Taquari were already about to threaten him with their weapons. But the words and piercing gaze of the big cat calmed them down. They fearlessly followed him. As they reached the top, they found out, horrified, that the sacred alcove had been walled up to prevent Coki from escaping. The sealing stone blocks were enormous. For the air and the food to go through, only a narrow opening had been left.

Then, Jiboia the anaconda appeared. Before the astonished gazes of Tali Nohkati and Taquari, the reptile swayed his whole body. Armed with incredible strength, he entered the enclosed chamber and pushed out the blocks one by one. A violent wind started to blow. The thunder rumbled. A terrible storm fell on the city, thus covering the echo of the destruction.

Coki was freed and taken away by the men of her life as quickly as lightning. Covering their escape, Yaguara and Jiboia, the two kings of the forest, saw that nobody would chase after them. Ferocious guardians, they watched under the tormented sky so that nobody would disturb the eternal round dance of the cycles and destinies.

Run away. Run away as fast as possible.

Under the pouring rain, Coki, Taquari and Tali Nohkati ran until out of breath. The forest, so close, stretched out its long arms for them. Before long, it swallowed their bodies, gulping them down to the depths of its bowels. Its liana, branches, leaves covered their mad run. Its animals friendly lit up their eyes aglow, thus marking out the rain-soaked trails. Soon, a new day dawned but, under the trees, the light could barely be seen.

They rested for a while and then set out again. Another day dawned. Another one again that took them through a narrow plain when, all of a sudden, a high mountain rose before them. Covered in snow, this magnificent wall of stones and rocks blocked out the horizon, stretched to infinity. It was breathtaking.

But already, dusk wrapped around them. Darkness would soon mask the paths, and it would become impossible to keep on walking.

Suddenly, a majestic condor landed by their side. Stunned, Coki, Taquari and Tali Nohkati looked at him.

"Here, the mountain reigns supreme. I, Colca, am its guardian," the bird said, in a strange voice.

Exhausted by their journey, without any hope of returning, they stood still, speechless. The bird invited them to follow him to find shelter in the mineral chaos. They did, both astounded and docile. A deep cave provided them with a safe shelter right away. Scattered scrubs were set for a salutary fire that warmed up their aching limbs.

Finally, Colca spread his wings. As a proud guardian, he shielded them during the whole night against the assaults of the wind and of anguish. The coolness of early dawn woke up Tali Nohkati. The same coolness as a long time ago, the same pure sky. He was young then. The attack from a tribe from the North had forced him to run away, with the clan of Rakenika, towards high mountains.

Just like today. But today, there was no clan anymore. There were no people of Caney anymore. There were only Coki, his beloved daughter and Taquari.

"Here, nobody will come and look for you," the condor told him. "See how the land is dry and rocky. Nobody can live on these high plateaus, battered by the wind."

"Then, we will leave and the sooner, the better," Tali Nohkati answered.

"The fertile lands are far far away. Winter is arriving. The cold will break your last strength."

"We don't really have a choice," Taquari let out as he joined them.

The condor scanned the horizon and said:

"Then, you will follow my shadow as I fly, the shadow of my wings. I will guide you through the dangerous crests. I will point out the game to you, as it is very scarce in this region."

These words upset Tali Nohkati, bringing him back to the uncertain time of his childhood.

First, Atii the whale had kept him in her belly to cross the white sea. Then, Raven the crow had protected Nuttah. Of her, he used to tenderly say: "My daughter of the North, my dear whom I have seen be born."

It was as if everything started again. Then, he recalled the words of those who had joined the big city: "There is, they said, an impassable mountain where only eagles live. There are signs on the ground, drawn by an army of giants. There is a mysterious temple, long ago abandoned, that brushes the sky. And even further, there is a big ocean, so vast that nobody will ever dare cross it."

Coki inched closer. She had just woken up and happily breathed the light and pure air. On her lips, a smile hovered. She took the hands of her husband and those of her father. She put them on her belly. In her eyes, all the promises of the world sparkled.

The life that was springing in her made their heart race and, under the protection of Colca, they set off. All along their journey, danger was omnipresent. Without the help of Colca, they would have gotten lost in the narrow paths and the fog. They would have been killed by masses of fallen rocks.

In this deserted region, men had left gigantic marks on the ground. Through them, did they want to call the Gods? Did they hope for a sign from the hereafter?

But the condor pushed them to climb up the high plateau, where the grass was green, where rivers flowed. They would then come across with abandoned villages. But since when? It seemed that those who lived there before had left only yesterday.

After setting up the fruit of their hunting, Coki, Tali Nohkati and Taquari would take over a house.

In those unhoped-for shelters, they caught their breath and regained their strength. The hearths, for long out, were brought back to life. The lively flames kept them company and rocked their sleep. Coyote came one night by Tali Nohkati's side. The Moon, more beautiful than ever, came along and said:

"At the foot of the other side, there is a vast sea, deep and rich. There is a powerful and warm current that can carry you far away."

Thus, the world was even vaster than he had imagined. It stretched further, beyond the horizon that the eyes of men could not see. Tali Nohkati, who had walked so much, who had seen so many landscapes, and Taquari, who had joined them, listened to these words. By their side, Coki slept in the gentle warmth of the makeshift home.

Time went by, and already her rounded belly undulated in waves.

32 MUKKI'S SMILE

They finally reached the other side.

As they proceeded, they had seen far away, in front of them, fires in the night. Men lived in these hostile lands, yet they had not joined them, choosing to keep on walking instead.

In the folds of the coastal strip, they finally settle down. From now on, Coki could not walk anymore. Her heavier belly prevented her from moving too much. But the time of delivery came. Blanketed by the dusk of a starry night, she laid down, breathing hard, to give life.

By her side, Taquari and Tali Nohkati maintained a gentle warmth, transmitting all their strength to her; all of a sudden, the child appeared. As magnificent as hope, he wriggled about, already looking for the breast of his mother.

In wonder, Coki named him Mukki.

Wild with joy, Taquari and Tali Nohkati danced, laughed and sang: "Mukki, Mukki, beautiful child of love, Mukki, Mukki, now you have come to the light!" They could not stop looking at him, holding him in their arms in turns.

Days went by.

Coki recovered.

The two men had tamed their space. Hunting and fishing brought good catch. But the surrounding lands were not fertile. Carrying the child on her back, Coki picked up and grew corn and potatoes only on a few patches of land. Thus, they were torn with the desire to leave.

They often mentioned it when the evening fell. Because, one day, their solitude and isolation could be fatal, they would have to, sooner or later, meet up with other men. But the child was still too young, too dependent to take the risk of a long and perilous journey.

Therefore, they waited for the correct time, the right wind, the safe wave. They watched the sky, as they had long ago on the Island of Caguama. This island, superb and generous, often came back in their dreams and they wondered:

"In such a vast world, there must be other islands like this one. Some, there, talked about it." Yes, discovering a land like Cuagama would be wonderful. Tali Nohkati and his children really wished for it. But a mute apprehension gnawed its way into his mind. Which kind of men would they meet? Would they accept the four of them? What would they believe in?

To which Gods would they ask them to sacrifice their existence?

Tali Nohkati did not want any more sacrifices.

After all his experiences with men, he knew that truth was to be found in Mukki's smile.

Truth was in grief from loss, in the memory of Nuttah, Rakenika and Gaho. After having travelled across so many places, he knew that truth was in the myriad of stars, in the water of rivers and in the powers of life.

One morning, as the mists of the Great South wrapped around them and as a cold wind blew, they decided to leave. They knew that by travelling northwards along the coast, they would end up finding a more welcoming land. Day after day, they progressed.

Already, Mukki walked his first steps, talked his first words. Everything filled him with wonder, and his joy inspired his parents to keep going, more and more. At times, as they followed dunes, they could see footprints. Was it someone who got lost, who was shipwrecked? A man outcast by his tribe? Tali Nohkati and Taquari would then look for him. But they did not find anyone.

They paused for several days, gathered provisions, rested. The weather was milder and milder. The vast range of mountains grew fainter to the East. The narrow coastal strip widened, opening up to an evergreen vegetation.

It was not an island but the birds that they could see in the sky and the trees lining up the banks reminded them of Caguama. They kept walking further north.

Soon, the snow-covered mountain tops completely disappeared. The ocean, on the west, bordered the shore and spread to infinity. And, suddenly, another sea appeared on the east. The clear water delighted them. Wild with joy, Coki, Mukki, Taquari and Tali Nohkati ran down the gentle slope of the shore and leapt into the water. Just like before, like it was there, the water was soft and warm. They were happy. The Sun stroked their skins, warmed up their hearts. Before long, they put up a bivouac shelter, picked up the fruit from the trees. The earth seemed rich and moist, ideal for farming.

Like them, men must have stopped here. They were certain of it; other men must be living here. Nightfall gave them peace. In the light of the rising dawn, a small boat sketched out on the horizon.

They settled down there, willing to stay there for a long time, maybe forever. The presence, not so far, of a tribe reassured them. From now on though, they had decided to wait for a while, to watch them. In the forest, they had taken refuge and lived discreetly. No one discovered their presence.

Days went by.

They were together. They lacked nothing. Then, one evening, Taquari made a decision.

Tomorrow, he would go and meet the men they had seen. He would introduce himself, make their acquaintance. Coki was trustful. Under the shelter of the trees that had hidden them as they spied on the strangers, they had seen them without any weapons. Their children laughed and played by the side of the women. Already, Mukki wanted to join them and play with them. Tali Nohkati also was hopeful.

At night time, he went to a magnificent cove that he was especially fond of. It perfect arch gleamed in the Moonlight.

The child had followed him and, holding his hand, sat down next to him.

Together, they looked at the breathtaking scenery.

Mukki, curious, asked his grandfather:

"Where does the blue stone that I found next to me when I woke up, come from?" Tali Nohkati, surprised, hugged the child. His heart overflowed with love.

Then, the child asked:

"How was it, the world, before?"

It was the moment when the words of his mother, words that he thought he had long forgotten, suddenly came back from the deepest part of his memory.

"Before, Mukki, it was a long time ago. In those days, the Moon was alone in the sky and Coyote was alone on Earth..."

ABOUT THE AUTHOR

Koza Belleli was born and still lives in Paris. Author of many MG/YA's books in Europe and Japan, she makes regular appearances at school literacy programs. One of her books *Le Bal de Houpelune (The Ball of Houpelune)* was read on Radio Classique in France. She also wrote the lyrics of the song *Esperanza Irisada* (*Sao Vicente di Longe* album) for Cesaria Evora.

Thank you so much for reading one of our **Native American Fiction** novels. If you enjoyed the experience, please check out our recommended title for your next great read!

Hunting Spirit Animals by Pamela Hicks

Hunting Spirit Animals is a surreal murder mystery set inside a Native American tribal school where the young die, too soon.

View other Black Rose Writing titles at www.blackrosewriting.com/books

and use promo code **PRINT** to receive a **20% discount** when purchasing.

CPSIA information can be obtained
at www.ICGtesting.com
Printed in the USA
FFHW022352110419
51691795-57117FF